# LITTLE WHITE FLOWERS

Kathryn H. Beard

The characters and events portrayed in this book are fictitious. Any similarity to real persons, living or dead, is coincidental and not intended by the author.

Any reference to public figures and comments attributed to them are fictitious and were added to this novel for entertainment purposes only. Comments were made with no malice and with the deepest respect for the individuals referenced.



ISBN-13: 9798850219574
ISBN-10: 1477123456

Cover design by: Art Painter
Library of Congress Control Number: 2018675309
Printed in the United States of America

*This is dedicated to the memory of my parents,*
*Alice and Henry Lukens Hartz*

*When life gives you lemons, and fate moves you into the dysfunctional Nashville home of a current top recording star, make lemonade. The hard kind, where the sweet, crisp citrus flavors blend smoothly with some of Tennessee's finest.*

# PREFACE

*Little White Flowers* is a contemporary romance for anyone that ever dreamed of starting over and reinventing themselves.

Addison Albright knew her life was about to change. She was marrying the man she had loved for almost a decade. She had resigned her position at New York University and packed the last of her belongings from the small furnished apartment she had been renting in Manhattan. Change did come, much like the pellets of hail that slapped her face and left her eyes watering in New York's harsh winter months. She had to get out of town, fast.

Magnolia Harrington owns a highly successful business in Nashville, TN that places domestic help with celebrity families. She is Addison closest friend. Hesitantly she agrees to place Addison with one of her clients. Addison needs the time there to rediscover who she is and how to move forward with her life. She must draw upon her sense of humor, caring nature, and common sense to masterfully balance condescension, ruthless rising stars, obsessive fans, dementia, national scandals, and a multitude of headline making events.

Luke Johnson's studio walls are covered with the awards and recognition he has received as one of the country's most popular singers and songwriters. He is handsome, talented, and all you would expect a superstar to be. Luke struggles with trying to maintain the basic values that he was taught with the temptations of being a star. Henry Lukens, Luke's widowed grandfather now lives with him. Henry has lost purpose in life. He is often confused, drifting between memories and current events. Henry can be obstinate, mean, impatient, and aggravating. Luke needs someone to look after Henry to assist him with day-to-day tasks. He seeks help from Magnolia's company. When all hope is gone, Henry's clear-headed decision-making stuns everyone.

Miles Wilcox lives at the ranch and is Luke's closest friend and personal manager. He is a complex character. He does not trust anyone except Luke. He is sarcastic and condescending towards everyone, especially Addison. When he comes to her aid and helps her out of an impossible situation, she finally understands the loyalty Luke has for his friend.

Travis is the second most important member of Luke Johnson's entourage. Travis is athletic and well educated. He manages Luke's ranch and staff. Most importantly, he is the person Addison depends on for help with Henry. His personality is the opposite of Mile's. His handsome African American looks, gleaming smile and calm persona helps Addison feel welcomed and safe in her new surroundings.

# CHAPTER ONE

Addison Albright knew her life was about to change. She had resigned her position at New York University. She had packed and shipped the last of her belongings from the small furnished apartment she had been renting in Manhattan to her parents' home in upstate New York. She was marrying the man she had loved for almost a decade.

Change did come, much like the pellets of hail that slapped her face and left her eyes watering in New York's harsh winter months. It was not the change she had expected.

Addison felt betrayed, humiliated and angry. She was, for the most part, homeless, unemployed and completely alone in the Big Apple. Never in her wildest dreams did she ever imagine that this atrocity would one day be exposed on national television. Her friends were mainly the wives of his friends and teammates. Did they know all along? She could not trust them now. The only person she could trust lived hundreds of miles away and that is where she had to go. She had to get out of town, fast. She needed to hide somewhere. She wanted to be anyone but herself, and she wanted to live anyplace but there.

Her direct flight from New York's JFK airport arrived in Nashville, TN. What was she doing? She thought to herself.

Hopping a plane without even telling her friend that she would be arriving. As she pulled her last suitcase off the airport's conveyer belt a shiver ran down her spine. What would she do if her friend was not there? Where would she stay? Where else could she go?

The taxi ride seemed to take forever. She had tried to call, but it went to voicemail. A message stating that the mailbox was full was the reply. She tried to send a text, but there was no reply to that either. She noticed a billboard advertising March Madness that made her laugh. "If they only knew how much madness," she said to herself, shaking her head and trying not to cry again.

The cab pulled up in front of a large building that housed many businesses. *Sweet Magnolia's* was one of the companies that occupied the seventh floor. The receptionist recognized her immediately. After a warm greeting Addison left her suitcases in the front office and headed back to surprise her friend.

"Great security you have here!" Addison exclaimed as she peaked into the lavish office.

Maggie Grace looked up from her desk when she heard the familiar voice and gave a quick squeal of delight.

"Well what broom did you ride in on?" Maggie said laughing, as she got up to hug her longtime friend.

"What are you doing in town, and why didn't you tell me you were coming?" Magnolia Grace Harrington asked with her slow Alabama drawl.

"Your suitcase better be in your car, or already on the way to my house. How long can you stay for? Oh, my goodness, Addie Beth, I am so glad to see you!" Maggie said to her friend.

Maggie Grace was the only one in the world that called her

"Addie Beth" she thought to herself. To the rest of the world, she was "Addison" or more likely, "Dr. Albright". Even her parents rarely called her by her first and middle name. However, in Maggie's world, every woman had two first names, and if they didn't, then "Miss" was added. Today, hearing those familiar words, "Addie Beth," was like salve to her broken heart.

Addison smiled, still enjoying her friend's tight grasp that encased her body and quieted her soul. Her embrace felt so welcoming and heartfelt that it brought tears to her eyes. Addison needed to feel loved, especially right now. A flurry of new questions was already coming from Maggie.

Addison and Magnolia had been an unlikely pair when first assigned university housing together fifteen years earlier at the University of Virginia. Addison, Maggie Grace, Amanda Renee, and Evelyn Faye had been the original suitemates their freshman year. By graduation, only Addison and Magnolia had remained roommates and lifelong friends. Magnolia Grace went on to law school at William and Mary. Addison, who was multi-lingual, traveled back north to Syracuse University where she earned a Master of Arts degree in Linguistics and then continued her studies at Columbia University, earning her Doctorate.

Addison Elizabeth Albright came from a conservative upstate New York family. She never thought of New York as being her home, rather just a base to return to in between the government appointments assigned to her father. She loved going to Yankee Stadium with him whenever his busy schedule allowed them to visit NewYork City. She also loved the bustle of shopping on 5th Avenue, the Broadway theatres, and the performances at the Lincoln Center.

Addison's parents met when they were both students at

Georgetown University. Her father earned his Juris Doctor degree in law and her mother studied medicine.

For many years Addison's father served as a Foreign Service Officer for the United States. He spent most of his career overseas at various US embassies working on complex issues like immigration and refugee relocation. Addison liked to fantasize that her father was a spy much like the James Bond character she loved to watch in the movies and read about in Ian Fleming's books.

Addison's mother was a talented pediatrician, but her husband's constant reassignments hindered her opportunity to grow a substantial practice in any one community. Committed to helping others, she often volunteered her services in third world mission projects sponsored by their Methodist denomination. She would bring her young daughter with her during summer breaks from school. Between her parents' work and philanthropic endeavors, their daughter had traveled the globe extensively.

Addison was taught that the many privileges she was fortunate to grow up with, came with a responsibility to help others. Before coming to Nashville, she had just finished a project with the Henry Street Settlement on the Lower East Side of New York City. She was fluent in Spanish and had been helping with an afterschool tutoring program for students whose English was not their native language. She felt a strong sense of fulfillment helping others and it kept her grounded.

Magnolia Grace Harrington was raised in Huntsville, Alabama. Her father had been a young NASA engineer that had worked on the Saturn V rocket series at the Marshall Space Flight Center. He helped to design the Skylab space station. It weighed

77.5 tons and was nine stories tall. He was on the team in 1979 that had been sent to Esperance, Australia to try to collect some of the remains of the space station after it crashed on July 12$^{th}$.

Magnolia's mother, twelve years younger than her husband, was a traditional southern belle. She had been a member of the Junior League, The Daughters of the American Revolution, chaired the local chapter of the Welcome Wagon committee and was well recognized for the numerous garden parties and charity socials that she hosted. She socially balanced out the introverted tendencies of her husband.

Magnolia was a clear mixture of both. She had her mother's beauty and social graces, but beneath the surface, she had an analytical mind that could calculate like a human computer. This had greatly benefited her in business. Competitors taken in by her charm never saw the takeovers and repositioning of their companies until it was too late.

In contrast, Addison was quiet and demurer. She did not hesitate to stand up for causes that she supported but imagined the worlds she would conquer would be through education and service. She did not need to be the center of attention, nor did she want to live in any spotlight. Magnolia had decided that Bette Midler's hit song "Wind Beneath My Wings" had to be their song."

Addison was a natural beauty who preferred to wear very little make-up. Her daily routine used only a light tinted moisturizer that had sunblock, a natural shade of lipstick and a little mascara. Her slender frame looked great in the relaxed and comfortable clothing styles that she preferred. She had an infectious smile, deep blue eyes and the layers in her long brown hair seemed to dance across her neckline each time she turned her head. She accented the neutral colors of her wardrobe palette with a colorful accessory or piece or jewelry. Living in New York City, she walked a great deal, and preferred to wear flats. She liked the good arch support that her Caroll Ballet Flats by Vionic gave her and her sandals by San Antonio Shoes.

Maggie Grace on the other hand, was a full-blown Dolly Parton with big hair, long eyelash extensions and bright tight-fitting clothes that accentuated her curvaceous body. The look served her well. The business she had opened in Nashville, Tennessee placed domestic help with celebrity families. Cooks, caregivers, nannies, drivers, whatever was needed to keep the mansions running smoothly and the celebrities out of the tabloids, and sometimes out of rehab.

Magnolia personally vetted her employees and working with her team of lawyers, oversaw the contractual negotiations and the confidentiality agreements. Her company had initially focused on country singing artists and their farms and estates in Brentwood, Tennessee. She expanded her business as football players from the Tennessee Titans began to purchase properties for their families to stay in during the NFL season. Now, because of her exceptional business acumen, her company had grown to include political leaders, pop artists, sports, movie and television personalities and anyone else on the east coast that wanted to protect their privacy.

Finally releasing the firm hug she had been giving her friend; in a subdued voice Maggie said, "Addie Beth, I am so sorry about you and Danny. You know I never did like ball players, especially Yankee ones. Maybe if you had dated someone from the Braves...," she said with her voice drifting off, not really knowing how to comfort her friend.

"Hey, one bad apple does not make the Big Apple bad," Addison said, trying to smile, "and, the Yankees are still my favorite team."

Addison had met Danny Perez when he played for the Tampa Tarpons, a minor league baseball team that is an affiliate of the New York Yankees. She and Maggie Grace had gone to Florida for spring break during their junior year of college and attended some of the spring training games at the George M. Steinbrenner Field. After one of the games, the young women caught the eye of Perez and a few of his teammates at a pub near the ballpark.

Danny was Addison's first real love. They were both ecstatic when Perez was called up to the majors. Their life seemed perfect. He was playing for the Yankees, and she was teaching Spanish at New York University. They managed to keep their eight-year relationship out of the limelight. Danny felt that public scrutiny might be detrimental to their careers.

"Well, I hope they send that boy back to a farm team is all I can say. Now how about you and I find a couple of Margaritas with our names on them, and then head downtown to Kayne's?"

Magnolia wasn't really looking for an answer to her question, she had already made up her mind as to how they would start their reunion time together.

"Aren't you forgetting your husband and two beautiful girls?" Addison asked.

"Oh, they've got plans of their own, or they will in a minute when I call them and tell them I won't be home for a while. Jamie and Brianna love it when the pizza delivery man shows up at the door," Maggie told her friend with a laugh.

Before Magnolia could make the call, her phone started to

ring.

"Oh Shoot!" she said as she lifted the handle from its cradle, rolling her eyes at her friend.

"What? Another one? That man is going to be the death of me!" Maggie said waiting for the person on the other end of the phone line to respond.

"By tomorrow! I can't wiggle my nose and conjure one up you know," again Maggie paused. "Alright, alright, I will have somebody there. Word is getting out you know. The one he bit is thinking about a lawsuit and the cook quit a week ago. Yes, yes, I will take care of it." Maggie concluded the conversation and then hung up the phone.

Maggie Grace gave a big sigh. "Looks like I might be a while," she said. "You might just be eating pizza with Nate and the girls until I get this mess straightened out."

"What's it about? Can you tell me?" Addison asked.

"Henry Lukens." Magnolia replied.

"Henry Lukens? Never heard of him," Addison stated, with a look of puzzlement on her face.

Maggie Grace nodded her head in agreement. She then said to Addison, "He's the grandfather of a country singer. The old man has a bit of dementia going on, he should be put in a home, but his grandson won't hear of it. I am supposed to send over another personal assistant for him. Someone who will watch after him and help with some household chores and do some cooking for him," Maggie Grace explained.

"He is one of the meanest creatures the good Lord ever created. He has slapped, kicked and cursed at the domestics I have sent in the past, and he bit the last one. No matter how much money, I just can't get someone to stay. My reputation is on the line. They want someone tomorrow and I am going to have to pour through resumes and schedules to see who I can find. I think I might have to get someone from out of state that never heard of this man, and then I am going to have to get their background checked, fly them in and get them out there. It is going to be a long night," Maggie said with exasperation.

"Send me," Addison replied quietly.

"What?" Maggie Grace said with a look that suggested that she had doubts about her friend's current state of mind.

"Send me. I can do it for a few days, which would give you a little more time to find someone," Addison replied, trying to sound a bit more convincing.

"You would not want to subject yourself to that kind of ugliness." Maggie Grace told her friend, shaking her head "no".

"Don't you think I can handle it?" Addison asked, this time with more conviction in her voice.

"Honey," Maggie Grace began, "I think you can handle anything, you know that. But why would you? Why on earth would you want to be somebody's house maid and nose wiper?"

"I need this. I need to not be me for a while. Right now, being me sucks. Let me do it." Addison replied pleadingly, with an ache in her heart.

Maggie Grace stared at her friend for a few moments without speaking a word. Finally, she reluctantly agreed.

"I can certainly vouch for your background check without any worries. How is this for compensation?" Maggie scribbled a figure on a piece of paper and handed it to her friend.

"You have got to be kidding!" Addison exclaimed. "That is more money than I earned teaching at NYU! Do your people really make this much?" she asked in astonishment.

Maggie Grace laughed. "Sometimes more. Those celebrities will pay a pretty penny for their privacy, and I get a hefty finder's fee," she told her friend with a wide smile on her face.

"So, who is this celebrity?" Addison asked, no longer able to hide her curiosity as she glanced at the display of framed autographed celebrity photos that decorated the walls of Magnolia's office wondering if it might be one of them.

"His real name is James Lukens. You might know him better as…" Maggie Grace paused here just to keep her friend in suspense. She finally said, "Luke Johnson," gleefully waiting to see her friend's reaction.

"Luke Johnson!" Addison practically screamed. "T-h-e Luke Johnson? The super-hot Luke Johnson? The CMA Entertainer of the Year; Song of the Year, Album of the Year, The Male Vocalist of the Year, and all those People Choice awards Luke Johnson? Oh my God, you have to be kidding, right?" Addison replied breathlessly.

"So, you've heard of him," Maggie Grace said with a grin on her face. "But remember, it is his grandfather you are there to babysit, not him. There are rules to doing this kind of work, and rule number one is to be invisible. Do what you are there to do, and do not get involved with anything, or anyone, other than what your job requires. You got that, right?" Maggie said earnestly to her friend.

"I got it. I just can't believe it," Addison said, barely able to keep her enthusiasm contained.

"Okay, I will have my legal team get the papers ready tonight, while you and I are enjoying that steak. Fill out these papers and then we can go," Maggie Grace said as she took a folder out of a file cabinet drawer and handed it to her friend.

# CHAPTER TWO

After waiting what seemed like an eternity, the door was finally opened by a disheveled looking man who was wearing straight black Lee jeans, a faded Led Zeppelin tee shirt and Justice cowboy boots. He looked to be in his mid-thirties, about six feet tall, and had a solidly built frame with wide shoulders. His reddish-brown skin tones made him look like he had a deep tan. She noticed his high cheekbones and coarse straight black hair that had been pulled back and secured with a rubber band. One of his ears was pierced and he had a large ring on his right hand. Both pieces had turquois stones. The man's Native American roots were obvious, but she wondered from whom he had inherited his incredible steel blue eyes.

"You from the agency?" was the gruff greeting the young woman received as he moved aside to let her into the front foyer of Luke Johnson's home.

She thought that he might not have shaved in at least a week and as Addison walked past him, she decided he needed a shower too. She was also annoyed by the sleazy kind of way he looked her up and down and that made her feel a bit uncomfortable.

"You're better looking than the last one." He told her with

a half grin on his face.

He was nauseating, she thought.

"My name is, " she started to say but was cut off immediately by the ill-mannered man.

"I don't really care, and don't expect me to learn your name until you have been here at least a month," the man said rudely.

"We are in the middle of a jam session, so we will get to you when we can. Just wait here," he said nodding towards a stiff looking Hancock bench in the hallway.

"Don't touch anything," he added as he walked away.

Addison stood there in disbelief. The driver had just finished neatly stacking her suitcases on the front porch, and she thought about retreating to the agency car that was preparing to pull away from the house.

"What an ass." She said, not realizing that the words had left her lips.

"He's an ass."

Addison heard a soft voice parrot her comment.

Looking around she did not see anyone, until she noticed a pair of New Balance sneakers poking out from behind a curtain in the hallway.

"Great," she thought. "I'll be fired before I even get hired," she said to herself.

She slowly walked over to the shoes, still not able to see who was attached to them.

"I am so sorry," she said to the curtain. "I did not realize anyone could hear me."

"He is an ass." The voice behind the curtain firmly replied, "and he is the sorry one."

Addison slowly peeled the curtain back to find an elderly man staring back at her.

"Hello," she said softly, giving the older gentleman a big smile. "My name is Addison."

He looked at her silently for a few moments.

"Henry. Henry's my name," he finally said.

She had figured as much.

"Did they send you to change my diapers?" Henry said with a snarl.

"No, they sent me to assist you. They said you were very busy, and very important, and that I was to help you in every way possible," she said softly, smiling sincerely. He said nothing back.

"You are Henry Lukens, right?" Addison asked.

"Yes," was his reply.

"Then I guess you are my boss. They told me I would be working for Henry Lukens. Would you like to interview me?" Addison asked.

Henry straightened up a bit. "You work for me?" He said, sounding a bit surprised.

"Why yes, that's what they told me." She replied.

"Not Jimmy?" He queried.

"No, just you. To assist you with whatever you need," she said with a smile.

"So, you have to do what I tell you or I can fire you?" Henry asked, staring at her.

"Yes sir," she replied nodding, "That's what they told me."

"I'm hungry," he stated.

"Well, can you show me where the kitchen is, and we can see what we can find?" The young woman asked.

Without a word, he came out from behind the curtain, and began walking down the hallway. Addison took this as an invitation to follow him.

Henry Lukens was a small man with a few wisps of hair on the top of his otherwise bald head. He was wearing a button-down, floral print short sleeved shirt that had half hidden a faded tattoo on his left arm. The shirt did not match the blue plaid shorts that stopped at his knee. White crew socks covered his thin calves and his sneakers had Velcro straps that needed to be tightened. He wore wire frame glasses and walked very stiffly as if his body ached with arthritis.

"Here's the kitchen," he said as they walked through the door.

Addison stopped at the entryway.

"Oh my," she said as she perused the room.

The sink was overflowing with dirty dishes that had not been scraped, rinsed, or stacked. Take out boxes of pizza and Styrofoam food containers that had been delivered to the house were scattered across the counter tops. A plastic garbage can was overflowing with empty soda, beer cans and water bottles. She could see a laundry room off to the left with towels and clothes thrown around the floor.

"What do you think of this?" Henry said, drawing a keen eye on her as he waited for a reply.

She looked at him, and then at the mess that lay before her.

"It's terrible," she said.

She had figured him to be a straight shooter, and she felt like he was testing her a bit.

"It's not terrible," he said, his voice slightly rising and

his face turning a bit red. "It's downright disgusting. Nothing but a bunch of pigs coming and going from here. If I was 10 years younger, I would whip each of their butts and send them packing. Bunch of pigs and leeches all taking advantage of my Jimmy."

Addison looked at him, and then back at the mess in the kitchen.

"Well, we better get busy," she said in a low tone.

"Busy?" Henry snorted back. "What do you mean busy?"

"If you want me to make you a snack, I have to have a sink and a counter to make it on."

Henry looked at her, not exactly sure how to respond.

One of the things Addison had learned when she volunteered at the settlement house was that most people wanted to feel like they had something to contribute. Circumstances might not have given them the tools to know how or what to do, but when asked, and given directions, they usually responded and found satisfaction in what they did. The key was helping them understand why an action was needed and what the benefit of that action could produce. The young children and teens she worked with responded with rewards when they reached their goals.

Addison concluded that the best way to connect with Henry Lukens was to help him identify the problem, find a way to fix the problem, and then reap some type of reward that an octogenarian would enjoy. In this case, clean up the kitchen and get something to eat.

"I need you to show me where everything goes. If I wash, will you dry?" She did not wait for him to give her an answer as she began to walk towards the sink.

He followed, like an obedient child. She stopped at the sink and looked around the room.

"What are you looking for?" Henry asked.

"I was hoping for an apron. I like to wear an apron when the job's a big one," Addison responded.

"An apron," he repeated, with a look on his face as if he were reaching back for a memory.

Carefully she rinsed off the dishes and stacked them on the countertop. The dishwasher was loaded with still more dirty dishes but had not been run. Looking under the sink, she found the detergent and started the machine.

"I guess we will have to wash these by hand," she said as she ran the disposal and then filled the sink with hot soapy water. "Where do you keep the garbage bags?" She asked Henry.

"Over there," he said nodding towards the laundry room area.

"Could you grab a couple and start throwing out the cartons while I start washing?" Addison asked as she picked up the first soapy dish.

He strolled over and diligently began filing the large Hefty he had taken from the shelf.

"Looks like I'm on KP duty today," he mumbled as he stuffed the containers into the black plastic.

"You and me both, General," she replied as she turned to face him, bringing her left hand up to a salute formation.

She smiled as he laughed. She could see a slight twinkle in his eyes and the lines on his face seemed to soften.

"Only a private," he said. "Wasn't in long enough to get above that."

"World War II?" Addison asked.

Henry shook his head and said, "Wasn't old enough. Korea, 1951 to 1953."

Addison nodded. "My grandfather served in Korea," she told him.

"He was a good man then," Henry said, nodding his head in approval.

He finished sacking the boxes and drink containers, and then came over to the sink.

"Almost done washing." Addison told him. "You can help me dry, and then we can figure out where to put them."

"I'm not getting any less hungry," he told her.

Addison smiled. "What would you like?" she asked.

"Some roast beef, mashed potatoes with gravy, peas cooked in milk and butter, sliced cucumbers and apple pie," he said looking over at her to see what kind of response she would make.

"Well, we might not be able to fill that order right now, do you have a second choice?" She said with a smile.

"I would settle for some hot cookies and maybe some coffee to go with them," he told her.

Addison thought about her grandparents for a moment. She recalled how her grandfather always gave in to whatever her grandmother wanted if she approached the question with a batch of warm gingerbread or chocolate chip cookies.

"Let's see what's in the pantry," Addison suggested.

Addison was surprised to see how well stocked the pantry and the freezer were. With all this good food, she could not understand why there had been such a flurry of take-out containers.

"We've got a delivery system from the store, they come

every week. We just have not had anyone that knows how to cook in a while," Henry said.

"There is hamburger in the freezer, and sauce and pasta in the pantry," Addison said as she looked to see what supplies were on hand. "Do you want spaghetti for dinner tonight? Oh look, there is plenty of brown sugar, flour, and chocolate chips. How about that for cookies?" Addison asked, as she called to Henry from inside the large pantry.

"Start with the cookies," he said. I take a little rest around two, and I don't want to die in my sleep without having them."

She laughed. "Okay" she said. "Check the fridge for eggs and butter, would you? I think I will start a load of dish towels while you get them."

Thirty minutes later, the first batch of warm Toll House cookies came out of the oven. Henry grinned from ear to ear as he sat munching on them.

"Well do I get it," Addison asked Henry.

"Get it? Get what?" Henry replied with a puzzled look.

"The job. Are you going to hire me, Henry, to be your assistant?" She said, smiling at the older gentleman.

"I guess I'll give you a two-week trial. I'll let you know when I see how good your spaghetti is," he answered back as he picked up a soft chocolate chip that had escaped onto the counter.

"What is that smell?" a voice said as the kitchen door opened from the hallway. Standing there before her was the very handsome, very talented Luke Johnson.

"Good Lord, what has happened in here?" Luke said as he approached his grandfather, reaching out to take one of the cookies off the platter.

"I put Addie to the test," Henry replied to his grandson. "She did a fair job don't you think."

"Don't I think?" he said, turning his attention to the young woman in the kitchen.

Addison had just emerged carrying a load of towels that she had retrieved from the dryer and had intended to fold on the countertop.

"Well, who do we have here? "Luke said giving her a big grin as he walked towards her to help her with the bundle of towels.

"Addison. Addison Albright," she said, awkwardly reaching out to try to shake his hand.

"Magnolia Grace from the agency sent me this morning," she added. "My friends call me Addie," she said softly.

"I didn't even know you were here, but I sure am glad you are," Luke said with a smile. "Miles, did you know she was here, why didn't you tell me so I could meet her?" He said over his shoulder to the man that had left her in the hallway.

Miles was walking toward the plate of cookies, and Addison smiled when she saw Henry push the plate out of the young man's reach.

"Are you settled in?" Luke asked. "Did someone show you to your room, or take you around the house?"

"So far, I have only seen the kitchen." Addison said with a smile. "I hope you don't mind that I kinda went ahead and started right in." Henry and I thought the kitchen needed a bit of work, so he and I have been very busy."

"Pop?" Luke said, turning to his grandfather. "Did you help Miss Addie?" The handsome star asked his grandfather, with an amazed tone.

*"Miss Addie,"* Addison said to herself. Maggie Grace would be in seventh heaven if she had heard him say those two words together.

"Addie's gonna make spaghetti for supper." Henry replied to his grandson.

"Spaghetti," Luke repeated. "Well, this day is just getting better and better," Luke gave a smile and wink to Addison. She felt her knees going weak.

"If that's okay," she answered him back. You have all the ingredients on hand. Will there be three," she paused and looked at Miles, "or four of us?"

"Actually, there will be seven," Luke responded. "I have a few boys upstairs working on some music with me. Is that going to be a problem? Have you got any more of those cookies?" Luke asked.

As if on cue, the buzzer sounded on the oven, and Addison smiled as she walked towards it.

"Just in time for a refill," she said as she opened the oven door. The sweet aroma filled the kitchen.

"Those are mine," Henry said, somewhat annoyed now that he was not getting all of Addison's attention.

"Oh, come on Pop! Remember what you taught me about sharing," Luke said as he snatched two more cookies off the platter and handed one to Miles.

"Ok, ok, now get your butts out of here so I can have a few minutes of peace before I go to my room. I might choke or something if I gotta keep talking while I am trying to eat," Henry said acting a little annoyed at the two men.

Luke laughed as he led Miles out of the kitchen.

"Just follow the music, you'll find us. The studio is

upstairs," he shouted back to Addison as the two men walked down the hall. "Pop, can you show Addison her room and give her a tour of the house?"

# CHAPTER THREE

Henry Lukens' idea of a tour consisted of walking from the kitchen to his bedroom. Along the way he would point at a room and call out its name.

"Living room. TV room. Miles' room. Empty. Empty. Jimmy's Room. Your room. My room," was all he said as they wandered through the 7,000 square foot ranch.

"You figure it out," he added. "Don't know why we need so much damn space anyway. Waste of money if you ask me, but I am not paying the heat bill you know." He stated with a tone that altered between annoyance and complacency, talking more to himself than to the young woman.

Henry opened the door to his bedroom and Addison followed him in. It was a large comfortable room with many family pictures hanging on the walls. Even though there was a double bed, the furniture looked small compared to the room's size. The dresser looked to be about fifty years old and there were some rings in the wood left from wet glasses placed without a coaster. It was heavy dark wood with a wire-brushed finish. Probably oak, Addison thought to herself. The brass pulls looked like the finish was wearing off, most likely from years of use. The matching dresser had eleven drawers. The attached mirror was framed with tiny shelves that ranged from four to six inches in width. Each tiny shelf held a small knickknack. There were a couple of Hummel figurines, an ornate porcelain ring box, and a small brass dish that held coins and a pocketknife.

"My Alice picked that out," Henry said noticing Addison's glance towards the dresser. "That's her there," he said, pointing at a picture on the wall.

Addison walked over to the picture. She recognized a much younger Henry standing with a pretty, middle-aged woman and a young man in a uniform. It was a black and white picture, so she could not be sure of the woman's hair color. Was it blond, or turning gray, Addison wondered to herself. In the photo, Henry was wearing a striped, button-down shirt, and a thin tie. No jacket. It looked like she was wearing a wrap dress with multiple colors suitable for church, and there was something familiar looking about the young man in the Army uniform.

Henry came up and stood next to Addison.

"1983," Henry said. That's the day our John graduated from boot camp. My Alice was so proud of him. I was too," he said. Addison noticed a few tears forming in the older gentleman's eyes.

"She is very pretty," Addison softly told Henry as she gently touched his arm. "Your son looks really handsome too. Is that Luke's father?"

Henry nodded yes. He then traced their faces with his finger and muttered more to himself than to Addison, "Yes, that was a long time ago. They are waiting for me, you know, they have been waiting a long time. Won't be too much longer," he said as he stared at the photos, his voice projecting a mood of melancholy.

Addison looked around the room and tried to think of something to say to turn the conversation.

"Where do those doors go?" she asked Henry.

He walked over to one and opened it. She followed.

"This here is the bathroom," Henry said. "I never use the tub; afraid I will get in and not be able to get out. I take a shower," he said pointing to the stall.

The room was beautifully tiled with strategically placed grab bars around the tub, shower, toilet and the wall walking into the room. It had a large double sink vanity and a linen closet stacked with towels and other toiletries.

"That there, is my closet," Henry said pointing to another closed door.

Addison opened the door. She was surprised at the size of the closet and the few articles of clothing in it. Her quick glance settled on two dark suits, a couple of white dress shirts, a number of Dickey tan-colored pants with matching long sleeve shirts, a few pairs of bib overalls, about six pairs of jeans, and a number of short sleeve shirts.

There was an assortment of t-shirts hanging up and Bermuda shorts. A shoe rack held six pairs of New Balance sneakers, and there were several short and tall boots lined up against one wall. Most of them looked like they had never been worn. Addison smiled at Henry as she shut the door.

"Help me get my shoes off," Henry said sitting on the side of the bed. "I am feeling a little stiff today," he added.

Addison helped him remove his sneakers and pulled the blanket up to the top of his shoulders when he laid down.

"I like a glass of water on my nightstand and pull those

damn curtains. I can't sleep if it's bright out," Henry added.

Addison fulfilled his request, and then stepped out of the room. She went across the hallway and opened the door to what Henry had indicated was to be her room. She was overwhelmed when she saw it. The bedroom suite was bigger than the apartment on E 10$^{th}$ Street in Greenwich Village that Addison had occupied when she had lived and worked in New York City.

There was a beautiful Hinkle Harris cherry, king size bed, luxuriously fitted with an assortment of decorative pillows. She next noticed the matching armoire, tall gentleman's chest and triple dresser with mirror. Matching nightstands were on each side of the bed. A cushioned bench was at the foot of the bed.

A flatscreen TV was mounted on the wall opposite the bed. Along one of the walls was a computer desk with a plush leather chair. A small sofa and two wingback chairs were near a double-hung window. There was a huge walk-in closet, a side dressing room and a complete bath with tub, shower stall, double sink vanity, toilet and a bidet.

Next to the dressing room was a small kitchenette area. She opened the two cherry base cabinets and ran her fingers across the cool marble countertop. Between the cabinets was a small built-in refrigerator. Next to that was a wine cooler stocked with six bottles of assorted reds and whites. A coffee pot and microwave were on the counter above one of the cabinets, and a small bar sink was above the other. Overhead were two small cabinets. One held an assortment of glasses and dishes. The other cabinet had coffee, filters, tea bags and cocoa packets along with a variety of packaged snacks.

"I have died and gone to heaven. I could live in this room for the rest of my life, and never need anything," she said to herself.

After seeing her room, she set out to explore the rest of the house. She wanted to open the doors to Luke and Miles's rooms but thought it would be inappropriate to do so. She looked in the rooms Henry had labeled "empty" and found, other than the color scheme, that they were very similar to her room. She explored the living room, the gathering room, the small and large dining rooms, the library and she opened the door to what looked like a rather cluttered office that she did not enter.

Addison had been astounded by the artwork that lined the halls and decorated the walls. Upon close examination she found an incredible Southwestern themed painting of a deer skull by Georgia O'Keeffe hanging in the giant gathering room situated between the mounted heads of a large twelve-point mule deer, and a magnificent elk. On the opposite wall was a beautiful textile piece that had been created by Faith Wildling. The colors were majestic and bold. She thought that there was a bit of irony that the work of an eco-feminist activist like Wildling would mirror the primal instincts that were displayed on the opposite wall.

In the hall between the dining room and the library were paintings by Camilla Engstrom. Her pictures were bright, vibrant and radiated joy. Her signature creation, "Husa" could be seen in one of them.

In the music room was an avant-garde painting done by Lido Iacopetti. Addison appreciated how Iacopetti wanted his art to be accessible to the general public and often displayed it in schools and hospitals. She had purchased a calendar at Christmas for her mother that featured reproductions of the artist's work.

The previous year, she and her mother had flown to Buenos Aires for a vacation while Addison was on hiatus during the summer session at New York University. A highlight of their trip was attending an exhibition of Iacopetti's work at the Barro Gallery. She felt a tinge of homesickness. She last saw her parents the previous August before they left to spend two years in Australia.

There was a cozy corner of the living room that was designed for quiet mediation. She found a lovely painting by Matthew Fisher that featured the ocean, seagulls, tropical flora and a beautiful sunset. Addison had once enjoyed a display of Fisher's work at the Shrine Gallery in New York.

Addison liked the fact that Luke Johnson was supporting newer artist as well as established giants like O'Keeffe. She noted as she meandered through the impressive home that there was a general theme of nature throughout. The hardwood floors had a natural polyurethane finish, and the walls were subtle taupe and light grays. Depending on the room, the furniture upholstery seemed to be Chevron linen, leather, or suede. Some had floral prints, green and blue plaids or solid natural shades of wheat, corn yellow, brown, hunter green and peacock blue. She wondered what high priced designer had been engaged to make these selections, and if Luke Johnson had helped with, or even cared about what had been selected.

After the library, she made her way back to the kitchen. She had not yet ventured to the basement level that was supposed to have a bowling lane, a fitness center, and a racket ball court, or the upstairs where Henry had indicated that Luke and the boys were playing.

In the kitchen, she looked in the cupboard and found some

cans of tuna fish and proceeded to make a tray of sandwiches along with cheese and crackers, sliced apples, and a plate of the cookies she had taken out of the oven before Henry's nap. She placed them on a bamboo tray she had found in the pantry and added five bottles of water, and some Pepsi's that were in the fridge.

Carefully she ascended the stairs and entered the studio where Luke and his band members were practicing. They were happy to see her, and the assorted snacks she brought for them. Luke introduced her to everyone, and she thought they all seemed like a nice group of guys. Miles continued to sulk and barely made eye contact with her when he snatched a sandwich off the plate.

The studio had six steps that went down from the door to a recessed area where a large console, filled with various technologies and recording devices was located. The walls of the room were decorated with framed gold and platinum looking records, seven Grammy's and an assortment of statuettes and awards from the CMA, Billboard, iHeartRadio, CMT, and various entertainment associations. Memorabilia from Mercury, A& M, Capitol and other record companies were also framed as well as photos from different venues where Luke had performed. There was a framed tour poster from last season that included photos of all the band members. Luke, the guys here today, the two women vocalists, one of whom was also an incredible violinist and drummer, and two more male members. Each has signed the poster before it was framed. Stools and instruments dotted the center of the room along with a beautiful black baby grand piano.

The room was soundproof, and she noticed that there

were no windows. There was a second door in the far corner of the room which she guessed was another entrance. She did not stay long. Taking the empty tray, she headed back to the kitchen to find the things she needed to feed spaghetti to this lively crew.

After dinner, Addison reflected on her first day. She felt that it had been very successful. She actually enjoyed it. Luke had rallied his musicians to help bring in Addison's suitcases that her driver had left on the porch. She unpacked and settled into her spacious bedroom and dinner was a success. After which, Luke and "the boys" as he called them, played and sang, which totally delighted her.

Luke and the band members played four or five old gospel songs that were Pop's favorites, and Henry seemed genuinely pleased that Addison knew the hymns and joined in when they were sung. Henry also brought out his "breath harp" and played an old timey tune for Addison's benefit. He ended the song with a few clogging steps which everyone cheered over.

"Do you play," Luke asked Addison as his band members started gathering up their possessions to head out to their various homes.

"A little piano but not well at all," she responded, blushing a bit to think that what she hammered out could ever compare to a musical giant like Luke Johnson.

"Well practice," Luke said, "because at the end of each touring season we have a little BBQ, and everyone that comes has to do something musical. The band is there, everyone that works on the ranch, my agent, and some good friends. Some of the fellows write a song or rework an old one and sometimes, we pick a couple to work on for the next tour. That's what we were working on today. The boys have some real potential hits, we were just tweaking them a bit," Luke said, nodding towards the men from his band.

"Once," he continued, "one of the wives, Imani, who is mighty pretty, and a big-time lawyer in town, but can't carry a tune, played *"Mary Had A Little Lamb"* on a kazoo for the BBQ. We all got a big laugh out of it, but she did it, and it was a lot of fun. I am going to expect something from you too," he said with a smile that stretched across his entire face.

"When is this going to happen?" Addison asked.

"Right before Thanksgiving. We try to be home for the holidays," Luke replied.

"Thanksgiving, it's only March. There is no way I will be here in eight months," she thought to herself as she smiled back at him.

Henry had moved closer to the conversation and Luke turned to include him.

"Looks like the two of you had a really good day today, Pop. Got anything special planned for tomorrow?" Luke asked, smiling at this grandfather.

Henry did not answer.

"He gets a bit quiet in the evenings, that's a good sign that he's ready for bed," Luke said to Addison.

"Don't ya, Pop," Luke said leaning in to give his grandfather a hug. "Now if Miss Addie needs anything, you're going to help her get it, or show her where it is, right Pop?" Luke said to his grandfather, who seemed to be drifting further off.

"Oh, I am fine, I don't think there is anything that I need," Addison replied, to break the silence. "You have an amazing home," she added.

Luke smiled at her, but then was taken aback when Henry

spoke.

"An apron. She needs an apron," Pop said quietly.

"Well okay then, we'll make sure she gets one." Luke replied looking at Addison and then back at his grandfather.

"A blue one, with little white flowers," Henry added.

Luke smiled and turned his head towards Miles, who had been listening to the conversation from a distance.

"Can you take care of that?" Luke said to Miles. "Get what Pop wants, okay? You know what I mean?"

Miles nodded, but made no comment.

# CHAPTER FOUR

Addison's window overlooked the circular drive of the 7,000 square foot home where Henry Lukens and his grandson, singing sensation Luke Johnson, lived in Brentwood, a suburb of Nashville, Tennessee. Luke's neighbors included Trace Adkins, Garth Brooks, Kit Brooks, Dolly Parton, Joe Rooney, Carrie Underwood and Trisha Yearwood, just to name a few. Many of Luke's neighbors, like himself, had secured the services of Magnolia Harrington's company, "Sweet Magnolia," over the years to find domestic help, cooks, nannies and private tutors for their children.

Addison was a light sleeper so the sound of a car pulling up to the house woke her from her dreams. She gingerly moved the curtain that encased her window and peered out to see Luke Johnson gliding into a chauffeur driven black Escalade. The sun had not come up yet, and when she glanced at the illuminated dial on her watch, she could see that it was only 4:30 in the morning. She crawled back under the luxurious white duvet that covered her bed.

I wonder where he is going, she thought to herself as her mind drifted off in multiple directions, fantasizing as to what his quest might be. Had he seen her? Was he thinking about her? No, he probably did not even remember her name. After all, they had only spent one evening together. One amazing evening, she thought, smiling and sighing to herself. She rationalized that the reality was, he only thought of her as another hired hand, which in actuality, she was.

Addison lay in her bed, unable to go back to sleep. Images of Luke Johnson that she had seen in countless tabloid and entertainment magazines filled her head. She thought about the photos of Luke riding a horse, his muscular arms holding the reins. Luke at the beach, his tanned body with an amazing six pack outlined on his abdomen, being splashed by three bikini clad girls. Luke in tight jeans, a button-down shirt that exposed his chest hair and a cowboy hat dipped below his eyes. Luke at a charity event serving hamburgers to homeless vets. Luke in concert. Luke walking across a field holding a small calf that had wandered away from its mother. From the photos, her mind wandered to the previous night with Luke standing next to her, and asking her if she needed anything, and talking about things they would do together months away. Addison rolled over and wrapped her arms around the oversized pillow that had been under her head.

Maggie Grace's words of "being invisible" and not getting involved with the people she worked with, also swept across her thoughts. Hadn't she learned her lesson from being with Danny Perez? They had kept their romance out of the public eye. Dating a celebrity has many pitfalls. She hated the way the girls had clung to Danny, asking for autographs and suggesting much more. The tabloids and weekly magazines often printed photos of Danny with gorgeous fans, at parties in various cities and had labeled him the current "bad boy" of the New York Yankees. Of course, Danny always dismissed the rumors, assuring Addison that he was faithful to her.

Don't be an idiot, she thought to herself as the feelings of betrayal, and broken heartedness swelled up inside her. She tried to quell the tears that had welled up in her eyes. A new life, a new beginning, she said to herself. At least she had not gone through with the wedding. She rolled over again, thinking now about Henry and his late wife, and her parents. Was she ever going to find the kind of love and devotion that they had?

Shortly after drifting back into a deep sleep, another sound shot her head off the pillow. She swung her legs over the side of the bed and ran over to open her bedroom door. She could hear an angry Henry shouting.

"I will not take my clothes off! Get your hands off of me," bellowed Henry.

Addison watched as a man in a white uniform tried to lead Henry back inside his bedroom.

"Glad to see you're up," were the words that Miles greeted her with as he stood sipping a cup of hot coffee in the hallway next to her door.

"Sleep well?" he asked in his normal sarcastic tone.

Addison glanced at her watch, seven fifteen.

"You never said what time the day started." she responded.

"It has, so when you get dressed, I will meet you in the kitchen. Henry's in one of his moods," Miles said turning his back to her and starting down the hall.

Addison quickly shut her door and jumped into a crisp, clean linen shirt and a pair of capris.

I'll catch a shower later, she thought as she quickly

washed her face and brushed her hair.

Her initial impression of Miles had not changed much from the previous day. He was sitting at the kitchen table drinking a large cup of black coffee when she entered the room. She poured a cup for herself, added some sugar and Half and Half and joined him at the table.

She noticed that he did not look quite as grungy as he had the day before. Miles had showered and shaved. Addison guessed he was about six feet tall, and his arms in the white t-shirt appeared more muscular than she first noticed. She thought that some people might consider him handsome if he toned down his obnoxious personality.

Miles made no attempt at conversation until she sat across from him at the table. He slid a pack of papers to her. Addison glanced at them, and then at him, waiting for Miles to give some hint of explanation as to what they might be looking at.

"It's a daily outline, contact info and general guidelines," Miles finally said. "I used to tell this to the personal assistants, but they come and go so fast, I decided to write it all down instead. You can read, right?" Miles said with mocking in his tone. "There are also some staff things we need to take care of," he continued.

Opening the copy, he retained for himself, and indicating with a roll of his eyes that Addison should follow along, they both turned to the first page.

"About Henry," he began. "He likes to get up around 6:00 and he expects breakfast by 6:30. Around seven we have a male nurse that comes in to bathe and shave him. He also records some vital signs, you know, blood pressure, stuff like that. Eight to ten, someone drives him around the ranch, he thinks he oversees it. That will be your problem. At eleven, he watches *Andy* on TV and most of the time he sleeps through that. Noon is lunch, two is nap time, four is a little more TV, dinner, and bed around eight. Have you got that?"

Miles had rattled off the information so quickly that Addison knew he had done that just to make her feel like she could not keep up.

"The next part," he tapped the papers, "is about the ranch. Here is a list of names and their cell number of who does what. You won't need most of this stuff, but you should keep it handy."

Addison skimmed the list. Ranch Foreman, Head of Security, Grounds, Horse Trainer, Pool Maintenance, Chauffeur, Housekeeper, Laundry, Shopper, Helicopter Pilot, etc.

"This list is about Henry," Miles said quickly flipping his page.

Addison followed suit, trying to keep up with Miles as he shuffled through the papers.

"Nurse, physician assistant, physician, drug store, barber, minister, sister, manicurist, optician, urologist, physical therapist, and personal assistant," Miles said as he ran down the list.

Addison noted that there was a name next to each of the caregivers, except for personal assistant. That had been blackened out and only the cell number remained.

"You're responsible if he needs any of them. Here's your cell phone, the numbers have already been added," Miles said as he slid the phone towards her.

"What about Luke's number, and yours?" Addison asked.

"They are in there, but don't use them unless it's a real emergency, like an ambulance or a hearse is on the way. And I don't have to tell you, right, these numbers are never to be given to anyone," Miles said sternly. "I also put in the hospital, ER, police and fire, just in case you can't remember 911," he stated with a condescending tone.

Don't worry, I don't ever plan to call you, Addison thought to herself as she gave a half smile to Miles.

"Here is a map of the ranch," Miles added, turning to the next page. Marked on it are the places Henry can go. He gets too confused if you take him anywhere else. He likes to stay on one path and have a routine. A driver will be out front at eight to pick you both up. Look for a white pickup. Henry likes to go over to the horse stables, and he likes to see the cattle. He also likes to hang around the barn when they are bringing hay bales in. He has a thing for corn too. He likes to watch them plant it, and he likes to just watch it grow. Crazy old dude," Miles said shaking his head as he turned to the next page.

"This section talks about your work schedule. When Henry's up, you are up. You schedule anything he needs, like his bath and shaving. When he naps, you get a break. You work every day, seven days a week. When Luke goes on his fall tour, the old man goes to visit his sister for about a month. You get that month off with pay to make up for the missed weekends. If you have an emergency, like a doctor's appointment or something, then you need to schedule the nurse to be with him. Got any problems with this?" Miles said staring at her.

"No, everything looks fine," Addison replied, thinking to herself that she probably would not be here long enough to take a month's vacation, she knew that Maggie Grace was looking for a more permanent employee.

"One more thing about Henry. Don't ever take him off

property by yourself. He gets confused and there have been some problems getting him to get back in the car to come home. Make sure you always tell security where you are going and have them send someone to go with you. It's best if you have a driver take you. There are a lot of crazies out there that want to get a piece of Luke, you never know what or who they will go after just to get his attention." Miles stated this in a firm voice, but Addison could sense a measure of urgency in this tone.

"I understand," Addison replied.

She had never thought about people trying to get to Luke through his grandfather. The thought made a small shiver cross her body.

"Now this section," Miles continued. "Magnolia's company handles your payroll and background check, but there are a few things more that we require."

"Ok," Addison said, as she glanced at the paperwork.

"We need a drug, TB and pregnancy test," he began.

"Pregnancy?" she said puzzled.

"Yeah, we had someone once who was pregnant when she got here. She wasn't far along so we did not know. She tried to claim that Luke knocked her up. It was a legal mess, proving paternity, tabloid trash and everything. Luke never laid a finger on her. So now it's just standard. You have a problem with that?" he asked.

"No, it's fine, just surprised me, that's all," Addison replied.

"The rest is just a general physical, and standard blood work. We need to have it for insurance purposes. You get life insurance as a perk. Never know when the old man might go off his rocker and do you in." Miles said this with something that sounded more like a snort than a laugh.

"He bit the last assistant you know, but don't worry we had him tested for rabies." Miles obviously thought he was funny, but Addison saw no humor in the comment.

"Anything else?" she asked.

"Here's a key to the front door, and one to Henry's room in case you ever feel you need to lock him in. There is also a security alarm system that is a bit complicated, so the next pages give you a step by step on how to operate that. Every room has an intercom system in case you ever need help. Oh, and there are cameras in every room and hallway, except for the bed and bathrooms.

The private living room we were in last night, and Luke's recording studio, have cameras, monitors and speakers, but Luke decides when to turn them on. He says he needs some space in the house that he can fart and not have it on camera," Miles said with his annoying laugh.

"Sometimes Luke will turn the speakers on when he's in the studio so Pop can listen to them playing," Miles added. "Henry's room has a camera and a monitor. We are not spying on him; we just want to make sure he doesn't fall or something. We also check to see when we think that nap time is over, you know to have the next thing ready for him. You can access it on your cell phone." Miles reached across the table to show her the app to use. He pressed it and watched as the male nurse was putting Henry's socks and shoes on him.

"You will meet some more of the staff today," Miles said. "Maria is the housekeeper. She comes three days a week and gets here at 8 am and leaves by 2. She is afraid of Henry, so she likes to work when the nurse is here or he is down at the barn. We don't have a cook now. Henry had a temper tantrum and threw a bowl of salad at her, so she walked out. Guess you will be making more spaghetti for a while," he said grinning at her.

"Got any questions?" Miles said looking like he didn't expect any.

"Where did Luke go this morning?" she asked.

"I meant about Henry and the job," Miles said, sounding annoyed. "Luke's schedule is nothing for you to worry about."

"I'm not worried, but if Henry asks me where his grandson is, I would like to be able to give him an answer," she replied.

That was only partially true, she wanted to know for herself, but it was the quickest answer she could think of.

"Yeah, I can see that" Miles said reluctantly. "He was going to the airport. Had to fly to Virginia to take care of some family business. He doesn't want Pop to know, it will only worry him, so don't say anything," Miles said to Addison.

"He'll be back late tonight," Miles continued. Just so you know, Luke is on the road a lot, even when he's not touring. He has TV, personal appearances, and things like that. He's about to do an endorsement for some jean company," Miles told Addison.

"Luke's weekends are Tuesday and Wednesday. When he can, he tries to be home then, and he keeps the house low key on those days. He lets a lot of the staff have those days off. Not you, you will always be here when he is, so stay out of his way. He needs the down time. I will copy you in on his schedule. There is an iPad in your nightstand drawer. The last page in the packet has everyone's e-mail info. No Facebook, Twitter, Instagram, anything like that while you are here, got that?" Miles said.

"I keep up with my family through Facebook, but I won't include any information about being here in it," Addison said.

Miles snorted again. "Great. Friend me, won't you?" he

answered in a flat tone.

Anything else?" he asked. "Henry will be down soon."

"No, do I have time to grab a bite before I get started.?"

"Yeah, and if you need to shower, do it now while the nurse is here with Henry."

Addison hated that she could feel herself blushing, she gave him a nod and headed towards the coffee pot.

# CHAPTER FIVE

Henry was on the porch swing where the nurse seated him when he left to visit his next client. The air felt fresh and cool and the grass was wet from the morning dew. Beautiful tulips, daffodils, grape irises and hyacinths were starting to bloom in the well-manicured garden that surrounded the porch. Addison reflected on how cold New York City would still be. Here in Nashville, St. Patrick's Day brought not only green beer, but seemed to awaken the earth as perennial flowers popped through the rich dirt and trees began to bud.

"I love spring flowers," Addison said, smiling at Henry when she joined him.

"What's your name?" he asked, looking at her with no sign of familiarity in his face.

"Addie," she replied, taken somewhat aback. "You hired me yesterday, we baked cookies together and sang songs last evening," she said, trying to coax some recognition from him.

He stared at her for a moment. "You need an apron," he finally said.

"Yes, an apron," was her reply as she nodded her head and gently touched his sleeve.

He looked at her and then at her hand on his arm. She

did not know if she should withdraw it or leave it there.

"What are we doing?" He asked her.

"You are going to show me the ranch. The horses and the cattle. That man," she nodded towards the pick-up, "is going to drive us."

Henry continued to look at her and then slowly turned his eyes towards the driver.

"The ranch, yes," he said, "we need to look at the ranch."

She followed Henry towards the truck. He veered to the left and approached the driver's seat.

"Get the hell out of my truck," Henry shouted at the young man behind the wheel. "I'll call the police if you don't get out, damn you!"

Addison stood frozen for a moment. She did not know how to respond to this, but the driver did not seem rattled at all.

"Mr. Lukens, it's me, Travis. I am your driver, remember? I am going to take you down to see the horses."

Travis Edwards was far more than a driver. Luke hired him to manage his sprawling ranch and to supervise the non-household employees. Travis graduated from Florida A & M University with a Bachelor of Science in Business Administration and a program major in Facilities Management.

Henry stood dumbfounded for a moment, and then slowly said, "that's right," almost like a little child giving into submission.

"Who's this pretty lady with you today?" Travis said to Henry as he climbed out of the truck, extending his hand to Addison, and giving her a big smile.

"I'm Addison Albright", she replied as she and Travis

shook hands. "Henry hired me yesterday to be his assistant," she said smiling and nodding at Henry until he nodded in return.

"Well, that is gonna make this ride even nicer," Travis replied back." Do you want to sit in the middle or in the extended cab," he asked?

"She's gonna sit up front with me, and I will bust your jaw if you think there is going to be any foolin' around going on here." Henry said in an agitated tone to Travis.

"No sir," Travis replied, "No sir, just a nice ride around the ranch."

The three started down the driveway that was framed with tall tulip poplar trees that were already starting to bloom. They turned onto a side road that led to the stables. Addison was in awe of the beauty that lay before her. The view was sheltered by the tall trees. The fans, paparazzi, tour buses and other gawkers could only catch a glimpse of the house when they tried to peer through the gates of the estate. All they could see, were fat lazy steers grazing on the fresh spring grass, not this majestic view that Addison was enjoying.

The stables could not be seen from the road. As the three continued on, a small aqua blue lake came into view. A beach area with a floating dock lay at one end. Further down was a boat rack with kayaks and canoes resting on the shelves. She guessed the little shed nearby held the oars and life vests or other items for the swimming area. Addison also saw a picnic table, a dock and some large all-weather chairs sitting on a grassy area near the lake.

"Mr. Henry likes to fish," Travis stated looking at her, then him and then the lake area. "Do you like to fish, Addison?" he asked.

Henry turned his head to look at Addison as he waited for the reply.

"I do, a little," she replied. "The lake reminds me of one my family used to go to in the Adirondacks in New York. I like the quietness of fishing, and feeling the sun on my face and shoulders," she stated in a reflective tone.

"I don't mind putting the worm on the hook, but I don't like taking the fish off the line, I need help with that," she added. "My dad would always do that for me," she told them.

Henry grinned and Addison was a bit taken aback when he reached over and took her hand.

"Don't you worry, I will help you with the fish," he said, patting her hand.

Travis had to turn his head towards the driver's window to hide the grin that came across his face. As Henry fiddled with the electric window opener, Travis turned towards Addison and said in a whisper,

"I think ole Henry is sweet on you," he said with a laugh.

Addison could not help but smile as she pushed her elbow into Travis' side and giggled. Travis was a refreshing change after spending time with Miles that morning. He had a broad smile, and she already liked his sense of humor.

Travis' had slipped on a pair of Dita Mach Seven sunglasses over his dark brown eyes when they started the drive. He had a moustache and a soul patch below his lip that connected to a small goatee. His cheeks were clean shaven, and his clear smooth skin reminded her of the rich chocolate hazelnut latte that she used to pick up in Manhattan at Starbucks on her way to work. She smiled to herself as she tried to decide which she liked better, the rich aroma of the coffee or the Creed cologne she could tell Travis was wearing. She knew from the jab her elbow had given him, that he had a tight firm abdomen. He reminded her of Shemar Moore, the lead actor on the TV show SWAT. Addison noticed that he had a wedding ring on and thought how lucky his wife must be.

The truck turned onto a brick driveway that came up to a lavishly covered entrance way. The stables, Addison thought, were more beautiful than some homes she had seen. The building was cedar sided. The stalls each had an exterior window with bright red shutters that complimented the brick pavement. She could see the faces of some of the beautiful animals peering out of their stall window.

A large white cupola graced the gray shingled roof topped with a horse accented weathervane. An ornate open carriage was parked near the end of the building. She could see five horses grazing in the white fence encased area next to the barn. She felt a genuine burst of excitement as they climbed out of the pick-up truck and stood at the entrance of the barn. She noted that the lines in Henry's face seemed to soften, and his breathing was deep and relaxed.

A few of the ranch hands came over to greet them and introduce themselves. Raymond, the man in charge of the horses and the stables came over with a hot cup of coffee for Henry and told Addison if there was anything she or Henry needed, to just let him or one of the boys know.

"Which one you working on today Pop?" Raymond asked Henry.

"Bring Rosa up," Henry replied.

"Rosa again? You got that horse spoiled." Raymond said as he signaled with a nod of his head to one of the ranch hands to go get the nag.

Inside, the barn was immaculately kept. The stalls must have been recently washed because the walkway still looked damp. Fresh straw, feed and water were available in each of the 30 stalls. Even the muck buckets were cleaned out. Henry and Raymond showed Addison the tack room neatly organized with rug and blanket racks, and various gear. It was obvious that Raymond valued his job, and truly cared for the beautiful animals he was charged with.

"We got a variety of animals here ma'am," Raymond said to Addison as they walked the length of the stables. "These six are Tennessee Walking Horses, the next ones are American Saddlebred. Jimmy keeps them for show. Then we got about twelve Hanoverian's that are mostly raised to sell and of course we got the American Paint. Those are Pop's favorite," Raymond said smiling over at the old man.

About that time, the ranch hand that Raymond had signaled to walked up leading a two-toned horse.

"This here is Miss Rosa," Raymond said. She is what we call a Tobiano Paint. That means she is a white horse with dark Davidings. Look here, do you see how her legs and hooves are the same color as her coat? Do you know much about horses, ma'am?"

Addison shook her head no, as she replied, "born and raised in a city, but, my, she is beautiful."

"Well don't you worry, miss, Pop knows a lot about horses, and he is going to be a good teacher, aren't you Pop?" Raymond said.

Henry smiled as his back straightened and he stood a bit taller. No wonder he likes to come to the stables. The men here treat him with respect Addison thought. She wondered if Miles had ever taken the time to come here with Henry.

The ranch hand wrapped Rosa's reins around a brass ring and handed Henry a bucket with brushes and other grooming supplies.

"I brought some for your friend," the man stated smiling at Addison.

Henry's eyes were gleaming as he petted the horse and encouraged Addison to do the same. Addison noticed that an apple and a few carrots were also in the bucket that the man had handed to Henry. Raymond tipped his hat towards Addison and as he and the other man began to walk away, he told Henry that he would be back in bit to see if he needed anything. Addison noted that Travis joined the two men at the barn door as they headed out to the adjacent pasture.

"Now this one," Henry said, holding up one of the items in the bucket, "this one is called the curry comb. It pulls the dirt up to the top. You start up here on her upper neck and you make little circular movements. Here, you give it a try," he said to Addison, extending the rubber comb out to her.

Addison moved closer to the horse. Henry gently put his hand on Addison back turning her so that she faced the rear of the horse. He then wrapped his hand over hers and helped her with the initial circular movements.

"You're doing great," Henry told his student as he moved to work on the other side of the horse. Rosa seemed to enjoy the attention she was receiving from both of her groomers.

"After we get the dirt to the top, we switch brushes. I like this one," Henry said holding up a stiffer brush. "It's made from goat hair, so it is stiffer but not too stiff. Old Rosa's hair is getting a bit thinner. She is pushing twelve now," he told her. "Now start back at the upper neck, we use it to brush her body with. You do it like this," Henry said demonstrating long careful strokes.

Henry and Addison brushed, talked, and laughed as they lovingly worked over the horse. When they each had finished, Henry reached into the bucket again and pulled out a mane and tail comb.

"We use this to get the tangles out, but I think I need to do it this time," Henry said. "Rosa can be a bit skittish at times, and I don't want to worry about you getting kicked."

Addison stepped back and watched Henry work diligently over the horse. When he had finished, he patted Rosa again on her nose. His face glowed with satisfaction. He turned to Addison and slightly jerked his head to tell her to come closer. When she did, he reached into the bucket and pulled out a long carrot and handed it to her.

"This is the part she likes best," he said with a big smile. "Now hold it out like this," he said guiding her hand toward the horse's mouth.

Timidly, Addison giggled, and let the horse take the carrot from her. Henry laughed and handed the second carrot to Addison.

"I think she likes you," Henry said.

This time Addison held out the carrot with a little more confidence.

"Now you." Addison said as Henry reached into the bucket and pulled out the apple.

Henry flattened his hand and placed the apple in his palm smiling as Rosa snatched it from him. Addison laughed and clapped her hands gleefully. Henry's eyes caught Raymond and

Travis walking towards them.

"Guess it's time to pack up our brushes," Henry said.

"Looked like you and the young lady were having a good time. I don't know who had more fun today, you two or Rosa," Raymond said to them.

# CHAPTER SIX

It was another one of those days when Luke left early in the morning. When she asked, Miles told her that he would be back late tonight. He didn't give her any additional information about where Luke was going or who he was seeing.

Addison had taken it upon herself to change a few things in Henry's schedule. She felt it did not make sense for him to start the day off with a shower and then do the barn work. He kept to his early morning waking, but a large hot breakfast was added instead of just the coffee and toast that used to be prepared for him. By the time breakfast was over, Henry's mind was awake enough to dress himself although she sometimes had to help him with his sneakers.

Addison instructed Stephen, the nurse, to come at 10:30 in the morning rather than 6 a.m., and to be waiting with sweet tea or lemonade for them when they got back from the barn. After a few minutes of conversation, Addison would point out to Henry that they both needed showers after working with the horses or whatever else they did on the ranch. Addison would tell Henry that Stephen was going to be on hand to help him if he needed anything while she was in the shower. She would joke with Henry about not watching TV or making lunch for anyone that smelled like a dirty old horse.

This simple shift in time and dialog made the experience less degrading for this wonderful man who had served his country and worked so hard for his family. Henry even stopped referring to Stephen as "Olaf from the Russian Mafia," and seldom raised his voice or shouted obscenities at him.

Addison recorded *Andy* so that Henry could watch it after his shower and personal grooming. She would watch it with him and then have him help her make lunch. For the most part, it became a simple, quiet, stress free routine.

Addison made a list of a few chores that she felt would be helpful for Henry's self-esteem. He talked often of the vegetables that grew on the farm he had in Virginia. With help from the landscaping crew, Addison had a small patch of grass, about 12' x 12' plowed up and she and Henry planted some tomatoes and cucumbers. It became his job each afternoon to water the plants and to hose off the front porch of the house. She pointed out how much cleaner the floors would be if the dirt wasn't on the porch to be dragged inside. Of course, there really wasn't any dirt since the walkway was paved and the porch was made of Trex decking, but it gave Henry Lukens purpose.

One afternoon, Henry and Addison decided to pack a picnic lunch to enjoy down by the small lake. To her surprise, Travis pulled up to the front door driving the carriage Addison had seen on her first day at the stable.

"Henry said you might enjoy a ride when you both were at the barn today," Travis explained.

Addison was thrilled and delighted. With a slow pace, Travis drove them down to the small lake and the three of them fished for about two hours. Travis and Henry had to help

Addison bait her hook and take off the small bluegills and tiny perch that she caught. Each were thrown back into the water.

To the left of the lake was a grove of late blooming magnolia trees, blushing with soft pink and white petals. They filled the air with a heavenly fragrance. Addison looked at the trees and thought about her dear and wonderful friend, and how lucky she was that fate, and Magnolia Grace had turned her life around.

Luke's spring tour had him on the road for most of April, so Addison started to take pictures of Henry during the day to send to his grandson. Luke seemed to enjoy getting them and found comfort in knowing that Henry was enjoying himself.

Taking a break at the end of the month, Luke's driver brought him back to the house about two in the morning. He quietly crept through the hallway, stopping for a moment outside Henry's cracked door.

"Johnny? Johnny? Is that you? What are you doing coming in this hour of the night? You be careful you don't wake your mother. What have you been doing boy?" Luke heard Henry hoarsely calling out to him.

Luke quietly pushed the door open and closed it behind him. The dim nightlights in the room illuminated a pathway to his grandfather's bed. He walked over to the old man and reached out and took his hand.

"It's me Pop, Jimmy," he said as he gently squeezed his grandfather's calloused hand. "Jimmy," he repeated.

Henry stopped for a moment and then slowly opened his eyes.

"Yeah, Jimmy, that's right," Henry said slowly. "I must have been dreaming."

"It's okay, Pop," his grandson answered. "I hope it was a good dream."

Henry smiled as his grandson still held his hand and nodded his head.

"I saw the pictures of you fishing, looks like you had a good time," Jimmy said to his grandfather.

Henry smiled and nodded his head again.

"You like Miss Addie, don't you Pop?" Luke said.

Henry smiled again and pulled his grandson closer.

"Can we keep her?" Henry asked in a quiet whisper, much like a small boy would do that just found a stray puppy.

"Yes, we can keep her, as long as you both are agreeable to that," Luke replied, smiling at this grandfather.

Henry smiled again, but then, pulled his grandson even closer.

"Where have you been? You smell like cheap perfume. Your grandmother would not like this," Henry said with an agitated tone.

Jimmy tried to hide the half grin that came across his face.

"It's okay, Pop." Luke said sheepishly, 'I had a meeting with someone that wants to sing in my band."

"Meeting my ass," Pop replied. "You don't need trouble like that. You need a good girl, and you got a good girl right here,"

Jimmy grinned and smiled. "She works for me Pop. I can't get involved with someone that works for me."

"Hell she does, she works for me," the old man snorted at his grandson. "I hired her. She's pretty, she's nice, she likes to go fishing, she likes horses and gardens, she can cook and she ain't one of those *fans* you keep running around with. Time you settled down boy!" Henry admonished his grandson.

"You're right Pop, time I settled down, but now we need to settle down and get some sleep. Okay?" Luke said as he squeezed his grandfather's hand one more time and then released it.

"You better settle down," Henry repeated as he rolled over on his side and Jimmy quietly left the room.

In the hallway, he glanced at Addison door. He smiled thinking about her, and some of the photos she had sent. For the first time in a long time, he felt that his grandfather had someone to look after him that genuinely cared about his wellbeing.

Luke saw subtle changes in Henry. There were fewer outbursts, and his grandfather did not seem to be as agitated and depressed as he had been in the past. He was thankful for the activities that Addison used to keep his grandfather active. He thought about the photos of Henry at the barn, with the horses, fishing, and in the garden. He chuckled out loud about the garden.

Henry had used his cell phone to take pictures of Addison bending over in the garden and weeding. He had Travis show him how to send them using the Messenger feature on his phone. Travis had added, "We'd like to grow a few more of those, God Bless America," to the message.

Luke stopped for a moment and pulled out his cell phone. He scrolled through the messages until he found the picture. Addison was wearing cut off blue jean shorts and a red and white striped tank top. Her brown hair was tucked inside a pinstriped Yankee ball cap. He could tell that her slender arms and long legs were starting to tan, and she had a pair of Pop's cowboy boots on that he never wore. Her sunglasses shaded her eyes, which he reflected, were a very pretty shade of blue.

Yes, he thought as he looked at her bedroom door, she is very nice, very pretty and, if circumstances were different, someone he would really enjoy getting to know better. He continued down the hallway to his bedroom. He decided to tell Miles to call Magnolia and give Addison a raise.

# CHAPTER SEVEN

Miles and Luke were just about to pull out of the driveway when a small fourteen passenger shuttle bus from *Gray Line Cares* pulled up in front of the ranch. They could hear the driver announce to passengers that they were now in front of Luke Johnson's home and then the driver started rattling off some of Luke's awards and the names of his biggest hits.

"Pull over," Luke told his driver.

"We don't have time for this shit." Miles stated. We will miss our flight."

"We always have time, and it's a private plane," Luke said as he opened the door and began waving at the fans who were screaming and yelling his name from the small private tour bus windows.

Luke walked up to the bus door and the driver gleefully opened it up for him. The name on the man's uniform was Ernie, and as Luke walked up on the bus, the fans were screaming and jumping in their seats. Luke signaled for the passengers to settle down so he could speak.

"Well hello," he said, "My name's Luke Johnson."

The passengers went wild with excitement. Again, Luke motioned for them to simmer down.

"I just had to stop when I saw that you were riding with Ernie," he said reaching out his hand to shake the bus driver's.

"You know he is my favorite driver that comes by my house," Luke continued.

Ernie was puffing up with pride and nodding his head, "yes," even though he had never actually seen Luke Johnson in person. He knew this would be a big boost to the tips he hoped to get at the end of the tour.

"Now I only have a quick minute," Luke said, "the fellows over there," he pointed towards the car, "are waiting for us to get on over to the airport, but when I saw it was Ernie's bus, I just had to stop over. You don't mind, do you?" He asked as the crowd once again yelled and cheered.

"Anybody want a quick selfie?" Luke asked making his way down the aisle of the bus, stopping to smile at an elderly Asian couple who were on the tour. Cell phones had already been recording his every word, and the passengers were straining to get him and their smiling faces into selfie frames. One young girl, about 14, was sitting in a row next to an older couple.

"Are you all together?" Luke asked.

The older woman said, "Yes, we are spending time with our granddaughter."

Luke smiled as the woman continued.

"She did not want to come on this trip, she thought it was going to be lame. What do you think now?" she directed those last words towards the girl.

Luke smiled and motioned for the girl to come over closer to him and her grandparents.

"Let's all take a picture together," he said. "Let's make this trip something you all talk about for a long time," Luke said to them.

He then turned to the girl saying, "You know, my grandfather lives with me. I wouldn't trade a second of the time I have with him for anything else in this world. You and me, we're pretty lucky to have grandparents that love us so much."

Luke kissed the girl on the top of her head and shook a few more hands as he worked his way back to the front of the bus. Before he got off, he stopped and shook hands with Ernie one more time.

"Hey, anybody gonna get a picture of me and my buddy and send it to him," Luke asked as cameras in the passengers' cell phones were clicking multiple shots.

"Well, I don't want to hold you up," he said as he got off the bus. "Plenty to see around here. Dolly called me earlier and said she was going to be hanging some clothes out on the line. Who knows, you might get to see her doing her chores. You all be safe now," were Luke's final words as he crossed the street back to Miles and his driver waiting anxiously for his return.

"I can't believe you do stuff like that," Miles stated flatly.

"They are fans, Miles, and fans is how we can live here, drive this car and charter a plane. I don't see how you can't see that I have to do that."

"I can't believe they throw down a hundred bucks just to look at fenced gates and cow pastures." Miles said with his usual bright demeanor.

# CHAPTER EIGHT

Henry had been acting a bit bad-tempered and ornery. He had been insisting for days to leave the ranch. He wanted to go out and do *something,* he wasn't sure what. An ad for the Nashville Farmers Market caught his eye in the local section of *The Tennessean*, the daily newspaper in Nashville. He pestered Addison to take him there, refusing to eat his lunch or shower unless she agreed.

Addison was not sure what to do. Both Luke and Miles were out of town. This was the first time she had been alone with Henry for more than two weeks without one of them being there. She was anxious and nervous. She used her cell phone to call Dale, who headed up the ranch's security. When she told him that Henry wanted to go to the Farmer's Market, he cautioned her against it.

"What could happen?" she said to Dale over the phone.

"It's a pretty big place," he replied.

"He's not going to take "NO" for an answer. He's really getting hard to handle," she confided.

"Well, it's your call ma'am," Dale answered. You better take me and Travis with you into the city. When do you want to go?"

"How about Thursday?" she said. "It might not be as busy on a weekday," she reasoned to herself.

Addison thought if the trip were a few days off, it would not look like she was giving in to Henry, and it would give her a few days to make him behave.

"Okay," Dale replied. "We better go early. Can you all be ready by 8:00?"

She said they could and hung up the phone.

Henry was sulking as he ate his breakfast. Addison looked at him and thought that in many ways he acted like a small child. Pouting and having tantrums to get his way. She sat down next to him at the breakfast table, bringing over a hot cup of coffee for herself and offering to refill his. He turned his body away from her and ignored her gesture.

"I am so disappointed with the fruit the market sent over this week," she said, as if she was talking to herself. "The strawberries were overripe, and the peaches were puny," she said aloud. "I wish there was a decent place to buy things like that," her voice wandered off as she took a sip of coffee.

"There is," Henry snapped.

"Really?" she asked, acting like she had no idea of such a place.

"The Farmers Market." Henry stated in the same flat tone he had used when she first met him hiding behind the curtains in the hallway.

"The Farmers Market?" Addison replied, as if she had never heard of it before.

"I've been telling you for days about the Market," Henry said, turning his body now to face hers. "Just like a woman to never pay attention to the important things," he said shaking his head.

"And they have strawberries and peaches there?" Addison continued, still acting like the Marekt was a new concept for her.

"Strawberries the size of tangerines," Henry said as Addison made her eyes open wide trying to appear amazed.

"And it's nearby?" she asked.

"Not far," Henry said, "just a quick car ride."

"Do you think we should go?" she asked him, knowing what the answer would be.

"Yes," Henry said, starting to get up from his chair.

"Not today," she said, I can't be ready today.

Henry sat down and gave a sigh.

"When?" he asked.

"Well, it's Tuesday," she said as if she was contemplating how to schedule the event. "We can't go today; Ray is expecting us to help with the horses. Tomorrow the barber is coming to trim your hair and nails," she continued slowly. "Do you think they are open on Thursday?" she asked Henry.

"They are open every day," Henry replied anxiously.

"Great," she said perking up her voice. "How about we plan on Thursday, as long as we get our chores done, and Stephen says you're fit as a fiddle. Should I call Jimmy and ask him?"

"No. You don't need to call Jimmy. I can make my own plans and decisions. I've had eighty-six years of practice." he told her.

Henry preferred that Addison use his grandson's real name whenever she talked about him. One evening as she helped him take his shoes off before bed, he even had told her that she could call him Pop as well. Luke had said that was a great honor. So far only he, Miles and Raymond were ever allowed to call him Pop. He laughed and said Miles rarely ever did, just to avoid being yelled at if Henry changed his mind.

Thursday morning came and an anxious Henry knocked on Addison's door at 5:30 a.m., a full hour before they normally got up. He knocked until she opened the door. She smiled when she saw that he was already dressed. Navy blue shorts and a yellow and white Tommy Hilfiger polo. He even had his socks and sneakers on.

"I've already started the coffee," he told her as he turned to scurry back towards the kitchen.

She chuckled to herself as she shut her bedroom door to get ready, still thinking about his outfit. He actually looked coordinated for a change, she thought.

Addison emerged an hour later, freshly showered and in a pretty pale-yellow halter sundress. She asked Henry if he liked it. She told him that she wore it to match his shirt. The May days in Nashville were already starting to get hot and humid. Her chestnut brown hair was pulled into a bun above her neckline. Addison rarely wore make-up, but always used Farmhouse Fresh tinted moisturizer because it contained a sunblock. She had used a fan brush to lightly apply some blush, and a rose shaded lipstick finished her look. She wore dainty pearl stud earrings and had a tiny cross on a thin gold chair around her neck. As impatient as he had been, Henry concluded it had been worth the wait. Addison was a very pretty young lady, and he was proud to be seen with her.

Travis and Dale pulled up about seven-thirty. She was glad they were early as Henry had been rocking in the porch chair at an alarming fast pace waiting for Travis to arrive. When Dale got out of the car, Henry looked annoyed.

"What do we need him for?" he said to Addison.

With a quick reply, she said, "Why to carry the strawberries, Pop," as she took his arm and helped him into the back seat of the Escalade. She went around to the other door and slid in next to him.

Nashville's Farmers Market was historic. It opened in the early 1800's. As they pulled up, Addison was surprised by the large structure. She had pictured it to be like the street markets in New York City, where a couple of blocks might be closed to traffic on Sunday morning. There, vendors used pop-up canopies to sell their produce under.

The front facade of the Farmer's Market had many windows, where the sun filtered through providing cheerful, natural light to the inside. A silo shaped entrance welcomed shoppers and homeless interlopers. It was located downtown and was a bustling attraction for locals and tourists. It had two outdoor open-air Farm Sheds where farmers, and other vendors, displayed tables full of tomatoes, squash, peaches, cucumbers, peppers and other produce.

Small kiosk shops and vendor tables were set up selling goods like pottery, small tools, handmade crafts, body oils, assorted candles, and fragrances. Vendors offered homemade jams and jellies. Fresh baked goods like cookies, pies, brownies and cakes were available. There were displays of bagged kettle corn enhanced with various colors, sugars and flavorings. Some vendors also sold bacon, steaks, roasts, and other meat. Tourist style tee-shirts with catchy sayings like, "Smooth as Tennessee Whiskey," were on display as well as a large assortment of costume and silver jewelry.

Throughout the complex singers perched on stools strumming their guitars and hoping that tips would be tossed into their cases. Some had amateur CD's available for sale. All had dreams of music row success, and fantasies about being discovered.

Rich and inviting aromas filled the air from the food court where businesses like Moose Head Kettle Corn, Farm City Coffee, Natchez Hills, and B&C BBQ invited shoppers to stop and satiate their hunger. Outside, food trucks offered a variety of choices as well. There was a giant, well stocked international grocery store within the complex.

Another popular area was the garden center. Rows and rows of vegetable plants, flowering annuals and perennials, small and large bushes, seedling trees and hanging baskets were on display. Garden furniture, products for pets and fishponds, wild bird seed and decorative bird houses were also for sale. One vendor had giant patio pottery, designed to look like faces, on display with the feathery and leafy fronds of lush green ferns billowing over the side.

The market often attached over 2,000 patrons a day. The rows and aisles were filled with lingering shoppers examining the vendor wares, baby strollers and frantic parents trying to keep up with their toddlers who were often distracted by the leashed dogs that owners paraded through the market. It would be easy to get separated from your party.

When Addison saw the size of the market and the huge crowd that had already poured in, her heart began racing. She wondered if this had really been a good decision. Henry on the other hand, was beaming.

"Stay close," she whispered to Dale as he helped Henry and

her out of the car.

Travis was going to park the car and catch up with them. He and Dale would coordinate their locations via cell phone.

The four walked around the first building of the market together. Henry really seemed to be enjoying himself. He had stopped to talk to a few of the merchants and insisted on buying a small bracelet for Addison. It was a silver band that had a small charm painted like a daisy.

About an hour into their adventure, they stopped in front of a large "I (heart) NASH" sign that was painted in red. Addison asked Henry to stand by it so that she could take his picture. He gladly obliged her, and then he told Dale to take a picture of him and Addison together. Dale fumbled with the cell phone but eventually took the photo. Henry told Dale that he wanted him to take a picture of just Addison. Dale again agreed. What happened next created a great deal of confusion and consternation.

As Addison was posing, a group of about fifteen people walked by, closely followed by twins in a double stroller being pushed by a man with a dog on a leash. Somehow Henry got tangled up with the crowd and pushed along some distance, before Addison, Dale and Travis realized that he was no longer with them. Henry took full advantage of his newfound freedom. He started dashing further away, looking back over his shoulder at the mounting distance between him and the others. He was laughing and feeling like this was a great joke.

Dale and Travis instantly went running after him, which only made Henry pick up his pace and trot off faster. Addison was following behind. She tried calling him on his cell phone, but he would not answer. She was panicking. What would happen if Henry got lost, or worse, injured? What would Luke say? Why hadn't she listened to Dale when he warned her against this? What had she been thinking!

The three of them reached an intersection in the building that branched off in multiple directions.

"What do we do now?" Dale asked, looking at Addison and Travis. "Should we separate?"

Addison looked at the area around her.

"I've got an idea," she said. "Henry is loving this chase, right?"

Both Travis and Dale nodded in agreement.

"See that bench over there?" she asked.

The two men followed her stare, again nodding.

"I am going to pretend that I have fainted. Dale, can you catch me and carry me over to that bench, and then act like you are fanning me?" she asked. "I think that will slow down Pop, I know he is watching us."

Dale whispered that he understood the plan. He handed Travis the bags of berries and peaches that he had been carrying and on cue, Addison slumped into his arms. He carried her to the bench, telling the people around them to please move out of his way, his friend had fainted.

A small crowd gathered around her as he tried to revive her. The plan was working. At first Henry seemed to not realize what had happened. Travis whispered that he had just seen Henry peak out from around a display watching them. Henry's grin on his face turned to a look of concern as he watched Addie not moving, and Dale fanning away at her. When it finally dawned on him that something was wrong, he quickly came over to them.

"What happened?" Henry said with a worried tone.

"I don't know," Dale replied. "One minute she was fine and then the next she just dropped over."

A stranger in the crowd was holding out a water bottle and Henry snatched it from her hand, remembering to say thank you. He took the handkerchief that he always carried in his pocket and poured some water on it. He then gently patted the damp cloth on Addison's face as he called her name.

Addison slowly opened her eyes and, acting like she was not aware of her surroundings, said, "What happened? I don't feel very well."

She slowly looked up into Henry's face with an expression that suggested she was waiting for him to give her an answer.

"Don't you worry," Henry said to Addison, still patting the damp handkerchief on her face. "We're going to get you home real quick. You need a doctor?" He quickly asked her.

She lifted herself up a bit and took a sip from the water bottle.

"No," Addison said. "I think I just got a bit overheated. I am not used to such big crowds."

"Don't you worry," Henry repeated, and then turned his head to Travis. "Just don't stand there, get the damn car," he ordered.

Henry and Dale supported Addison as they walked to where Travis was parked, she kept apologizing to Henry.

"I am so sorry, I just ruined our day, I am so sorry..."

Henry tried to assure her that everything was fine. They had the peaches and strawberries they came for, and it was about time to head home anyway.

In the car, Addison caught Travis's grin in the rear-view

mirror. As they drove, she could tell that Henry needed to stop. Between the excitement at the market and his daily dose of Flomax she knew he was in agony.

"Henry," she said, weakly reaching out to touch his arm, "I am really thirsty. Do you think we could stop and get a drink?"

"Yes," Henry quickly replied. "Travis pull in somewhere, I need to get Addie a cold drink."

"You want me to go through the drive through," Travis asked.

"No! I'm going inside to get it," Henry snapped at his driver.

"I think I need to go inside too," Addison added hoping that Travis would get with the plan. She shot him a look when he glanced at her in the rear-view mirror. He then nodded his head.

"Mickey D's on our right," he said as he pulled the car into the parking lot.

Before it had barely stopped, Henry was opening the door and jumping out, racing towards the building. The other three followed behind him. When they got inside, Addison nodded towards a table, and they sat down waiting for Henry. When he emerged from the bathroom, Henry went up to the counter and ordered two sweet teas. Looking over at the table, he quickly changed his order to four. Travis got up and went over to help him.

"What do you think Luke's going to say when he hears about this?" Dale asked, a bit nervously.

Addison thought for a moment and then said. "I wasn't going to give him all the details."

Dale breathed a sigh of relief.

"Besides," Addison continued, "This is all on me. You told me you didn't think it was a good idea, and you were right. I really am sorry about this."

"A lot of people were taking pictures." Dale said.

"They don't know who we are, and I was careful not to call him by name," Addison replied.

"That's true," Dale said. "I noticed that you kept calling him Pop. Do you think he will say anything?"

"I am sure he will. I am also sure that he will be the hero of whatever story he tells, and I will just go along with it," Addison stated.

Their conversation stopped as Henry and Travis approached the table. After a few restful sips, they loaded back into the car and headed home.

# CHAPTER NINE

When Dale, Travis, Henry and Addison arrived back at Luke Johnson's ranch after a disastrous morning at the Nashville Farmers Market, Addison asked Henry if he wanted to watch *Andy*. Henry said he wouldn't mind watching a little TV but had something else in mind. He asked Travis to stay for a few moments to help him set up his show. Henry hurried off to his bedroom and returned with a boxed DVD set of *Walker, Texas Ranger* starring Chuck Norris. Henry wasn't sure how to switch the TV over to a DVD, so he asked Travis to help him.

Henry disappeared again and this time, returned with two glasses of lemonade and a lap size crocheted afghan that his sister Helen had made for him. He handed one of the drinks to Addison and put the other one on the small table next to his favorite chair that rocked or reclined based on what Henry wanted. It also had a built-in massage unit and it had two heat temperature settings. He then directed Addison to sit on the couch and he gave her the lap blanket to put over her bare legs.

Travis left the two of them once the DVD started. Addison was only vaguely familiar with the TV show. It was not something that her father ever watched. Henry, however, was a loyal fan. So much so that he kept a running dialog of who the characters were and what was happening. Addison concluded that she could have summarized the entire plot just from what Pop was sharing, instead of sitting through the episode.

"That's Alex Cahill, she's sweet on Walker," Henry told Addison.

"Oh no, those guys are in trouble now. Walker don't like nobody messing with Alex. That guy should not have pushed her around," Henry continued. "Watch this," he said excitedly when Chuck Norris's character, Ranger Cordell Walker came on the scene.

Addison's watched as Norris' character threw punches and kicks at the bad guys. In slow motion his famous Chun Kuk Do style of fighting sent a man twice his size hurling through a glass door. Addison watched Henry as he enjoyed the show. When Chuck threw a punch, Henry's arm gave a small boxer motion, when Chuck kicked, Henry's leg jerked.

"Told you those guys would be sorry they messed with Alex," Henry said with a triumphant voice. "That Walker, he knows how to take care of his women folk," Henry added nodding his head to himself.

A few seconds later Henry added, "You need anything?"

Addison thought reflectively. She looked at the half empty glass of lemonade that Henry had brought her, and the lap blanket that covered her legs. She smiled thinking that perhaps she was becoming one of Henry's "women folk" that needed to be taken care of. She reached over and touched Henry's arm.

"Nope, I have everything I need right here," she said sweetly.

Henry patted her hand and grinned. A few minutes later Addison noticed Henry's head falling back, despite his attempts to shake himself awake. Before the show ended his head was resting on the back of the recliner and he was softly snoring. Addison reached for the remote and turned the TV off.

Probably why the show didn't start at the beginning, Addison thought to herself. She then stretched her legs out on the couch and decided to take a quick nap as well. An hour or so later she opened her eyes when Henry pushed the leg rest down on the recliner.

"Gotta get some water," Henry said getting out of the chair. Addison recognized that as really meaning that he needed to make a bathroom stop.

"Ok," she replied pulling herself upright and putting her feet back on the floor.

As she watched the old man move his stiff body down the hall, she began thinking about the morning events. She shuddered a bit when she thought about what might have happened. She recalled praying that they would find Henry, and everything would be ok. Praying. Here it was the end of May and she realized she had not been to church since Christmas. Other than the minister's phone number that Miles had given her during her first week, no mention of church had ever been made. Henry certainly never asked about going. When he returned, she asked him if he wanted to go on Sunday.

"Church? I am not getting up early on Sunday morning to go to church," he said flatly.

Early, she thought. He gets up every day at 6 am regardless, she said to herself.

"But you like the hymns," she replied to Henry.

"I like it when Jimmy sings the hymns," he retorted. "You can go. Go sing in the choir if you want to, but don't count me in."

Addison was determined. Growing up she never missed a church service, whether it was held in the church at home that her family belonged to, a missionary hut when her mother took her on mission trips or a beautiful cathedral in the country where her father was posted. Church had always been an important part of her family's life. She reflected how disappointed her mother would be if she knew Addison had not been to church in over six months. She had even missed Easter services.

For a few moments she had a deep feeling of loneliness. It dawned on her how much she missed her parents and how long it had been since they last Zoomed. They had no idea what she was really doing, and she wondered if they would be disappointed if they knew. She realized how much Henry had filled that gap. He made her feel needed, and a part of a family.

Later, Addison went to her room and found the stack of papers that Miles had given her when she first started working there. She had tucked them into one of the drawers in the beautiful cherry desk. She found a listing for Freedom United Methodist Church in the directory Miles had given her with Rev. Mitchell's name written next to it. She called the number. A friendly voice answered the call and told her that the Reverend had retired a year ago. Would she like to talk to Pastor Rich? While she waited, she crossed out the old minister's name and wrote in the new one. She would be glad to tell Miles that he had made an error.

"Hello," a man's voice said. "This is Pastor Rich; how can I help you?"

"Um, yes, my name is Addison Albright, and I am employed and live locally. I am somewhat new in the area, and I wanted to find out about your services," she said into the phone.

"Well welcome! We would love to have you join us at any time," the man responded. We have an 8:00 - 8:30 service, which is mainly communion and a short message. There is no choir or children's message at that service. We also have a 9:00 service which is more traditional and our 11:00 service is very contemporary. We have a band at that service. We also have a Saturday night service two times a month and a midweek program for seniors."

"That's amazing," Addison replied, genuinely impressed.

"We try to have something for everyone," Pastor Rich answered. Do you have children, or would you or your husband be interested in our Sunday School programs?

"Not married, no kids," she said. "I work taking care of an elderly gentleman. I think it would be good for both of us to get involved, but he is rather reluctant."

'I understand," Pastor Rich replied. "We have a great senior's program each Wednesday. About a dozen gather from 11 - 1. We enjoy a nice meal; fellowship and we sing hymns based on what the participants request. More like a social hour. Gives our seniors a chance to get out and mingle a bit."

"That sounds perfect," Addison replied excitedly. "If I can only get him to agree to come out and try it."

"I am happy to do a home visit and tell him about it in person." Would you like me to stop in?" the minister asked.

Addison thought for a moment and then answered with the affirmative. He then asked where she lived and what the name was of the gentleman.

"We live on a ranch in Brentwood," she replied. 'His name is Henry Lukens."

There was a pause on the phone. Pastor Rich did not immediately reply.

"Is this the Henry Lukens that is related to Luke Johnson," the minister asked hesitantly.

"Yes, do you know them?" Addison asked with a bit of excitement.

"No, nope, I have never met either of them. They are both listed as parishioners, but I have not had the pleasure of meeting either one. I called last June when I arrived and offered to introduce myself, but the man that I spoke with said he would let me know if they needed to plan a funeral..." he said, obviously regretting that he said too much, and worried that he might have offended her.

"That would have been Miles, he is such a joker," Addison answered, trying to make it sound lighthearted while shaking her head and thinking about what a jerk Miles can be to everyone.

"Luke is away a great deal of time, and he is gone most weekends." Addison said sounding like she was trying to make an excuse for him, which she was. "I came on board a short time ago to be a companion to Mr. Lukens while his grandson is away. He and I would love to meet you." Addison knew that was a half lie, but she said it anyway.

By the end of the call, Addison and Pastor Rich agreed for him to come for lunch on Tuesday. Addison thought that after a morning at the barn and a nice shower, Henry would be too worn out to be rude to the minister. Over the meal he could invite Henry to come to the Wednesday senior event. To her surprise, the luncheon went more smoothly than she had hoped.

Pastor Rich seemed very nice. He was young, she thought,

probably in his mid-thirties. He had sandy blond hair; an amazing smile and he looked like he worked out a bit. Addison reproached herself when she began thinking that Pastor Rich would be pretty nice to sit and just look at for an hour each week.

She caught him and Henry laughing a few times and was very impressed that the minister knew who Chuck Norris was, that he agreed that the best cobbler was made with peaches and that he could describe the right way to milk a cow based on his experiences at his own grandfather's farm that was located in Buck's Valley near the Susquehanna River in Pennsylvania. Henry seemed pleased too. He even allowed the minster to offer a closing prayer when the meal ended and he agreed, albeit reluctantly, to come the next day to the senior event.

Travis drove them over and asked if he should wait for them. She told him that would not be necessary. If the event ended before one, or if Henry had problems, she would call him. It was only about a 20-minute ride from the ranch.

The church was very pretty. A white country looking structure that would look perfect on the cover of a collection of gospel songs. Pastor Rich had told them to come to the side door into the Fellowship Hall. When they entered, Addison saw that four, six-foot tables had been set with white tablecloths. There were six folding chairs at each table.

She caught the minister's eye when they entered, and he came to the door to greet them. Behind him were a gaggle of women talking loudly with each other. When they entered, the women all began to look at Henry and seemed to be directing their conversation about the newcomers who had entered. Henry seemed a bit unsure about his decision to attend.

After a short greeting, Pastor Rich held up his hands and

invited everyone to find a seat. When they were ready, he would offer a prayer and lunch would be served. Henry and Addison sat at the table closest to the door. Henry had the middle seat at the table and as soon as he sat down three of the women that had been overtly talking when they arrived, immediately sat at their table. One on his right, and two across from him and the other woman.

"I'm Polly," the woman that sat next to him said. "Those are my friends Jane and Shirley." The two women smiled and giggled and then repeated their names.

"Is that your granddaughter?" Polly asked, looking over at Addison.

"Yes," Henry replied, which surprised Addison, but she didn't say anything.

After Pastor Rich offered the grace, a team of volunteers came from the kitchen placing bowls of food on the table. The menu included Dinty Moore Beef Stew, small dishes of apple sauce, baskets of biscuits with assorted jams in small individual packages and finely ground coleslaw.

"I'm Polly," the woman said again, this time touching Henry's arm. "What's your name," she asked for a second time.

"Henry," he repeated.

"Is that your granddaughter?" Polly asked again.

This time, Henry said, "No, she lives with me and my grandson. I take care of her when he's gone."

Again, Addison was surprised by his response, but did not say anything,

"She's his grandson's girlfriend," Polly reported loudly to the two women that sat across from them. "She lives with him."

Jane then turned to Shirley and said in a loud voice, "She's going to marry his grandson,"

Shirley smiled and reached across the table and patted Addison's hand. "I hope you have a lot of children," Shirley said to Addison.

"I hope it's a little girl," Jane said.

"When are you due?" Polly asked, leaning forward to talk around Henry.

Addison's head was spinning. She could not understand how the conversation's direction turned so quickly, or the conclusions that the three women had jumped to.

"Anyone need more lemonade?" Addison said standing up with the pitcher.

Addison felt that she needed to escape from her luncheon companions for a moment and headed over to the drink dispensers. Pastor Rich was standing there. He smiled broadly as she approached.

"I do offer premarital counseling, perform marriages and I love to do a baptism, if you're interested," he said with a laugh.

Addison laughed too.

"It's all happened so quickly," she said trying not to smile, "I wonder if Luke knows?" she added, and they both laughed again wholeheartedly.

"You should have seen them when I first arrived, and they found out I was single." Pastor Rich said. "I was shown more pictures of single granddaughters, grandnieces and divorced daughters than you can possibly imagine," he said laughing again.

So, you're single, Addison thought as she laughed along with him.

Still smiling, Rich nodded his head towards Henry's table.

"I think you lost your seat," he said.

Addison turned her head and sure enough, Shirley had moved from the other side of the table to the seat Addison had been using to the left of Henry.

"What a hussy," Addison exclaimed with a laugh that she and Pastor Rich shared.

"You snooze you lose around here," he told her.

Addison looked around the room. She counted thirteen women and three men all seated around three of the tables. The fourth one seemed to be reserved for the minister and the volunteers in the kitchen.

"Looks like you are going to be stuck with the help," Pastor Rich said glancing at the fourth table. "Let me introduce you to the others."

The four volunteers that day included one of the church members, the daughter of one of the seniors and two domestics that, like her, worked for the families and had brought the seniors to the event. They were a nice group of people. When the others got up to serve slices of pie, Addison carried around pitchers of lemonade and sweet tea to refill their glasses. She felt good helping and thought that her mother would be happy to see her do it.

When the table was cleared, the volunteer from the church went over to the piano. She started playing "Blessed Assurance" and a few of the seniors joined in singing. She then played "Shall We Gather at the River?" When that hymn ended, she asked for suggestions from the crowd. No one used hymnals and the verses were limited to those that most knew by heart.

Various seniors requested, "How Great Thou Art", "What a Friend we Have in Jesus," and "For the Beauty of the Earth."

Pastor Rich then offered a few words of hope and told everyone how glad he was to have them there. He introduced Henry as their newest member and asked him if he would like to select the final hymn for the day. Henry took that as a clue to stand up, and in so doing, began to say a few words.

"I am mighty glad to be here today," he said. "I have met some really nice folks and I hope you will let me come back. I don't know many people in these parts. I am from Virginia you know," he told the crowd.

"Thank you," Pastor Rich said warmly. "What song would you like us all to sing next Henry," he asked.

Henry thought for a moment and then said as he stood there, "How about "God Bless America?"

Henry continued to stand as the pianist started the music. The other two gentleman stood too and a few of the women. Polly jumped right up next to Henry and slid her arm around his as they sang. She had a smile on her face like she had just won the blue ribbon at the county fair.

# CHAPTER TEN

The telephone rang and to Addison's surprise, Luke's name showed up in the caller ID.

"Did you see that hit by Torres? Just added another home run to his record," Luke said.

"What?" Addison's replied.

"Don't tell me you're not watching the game," Luke said. "I didn't think you ever missed a Yankee game. Are you sick or something?" he asked.

"No," Addison laughed, "but I will catch the highlights later on ESPN," she said. "Since when did you start watching the guys? I thought you were a Braves fan."

Luke laughed.

"What have you and Pop been up to? I called his cell a while ago, but he didn't answer." Luke said.

"We just got back from church." she replied.

"Church?" Luke said with a disbelieving tone. "Didn't you go there last week with him?

"He's been going to a senior's program they have there on Wednesdays. I gotta tell you, he is becoming quite the ladies' man there," Addison said with a laugh.

"I have to hear more about this when I get come next

weekend," Luke said.

"You're coming home!" Addison said excitedly. "That's great!"

"I always come home for Father's Day. Have you got any suggestions for me as to what Pop might need or want?" Luke asked.

Addison thought for a moment and then suggested a golf cart.

"A golf cart?" Luke exclaimed. "What does he need a golf cart for?"

"I think it would be good for him. They don't go very fast, and I would ride with him. It might make him feel better about not being able to drive anymore. It might make him feel a little more independent," Addison said to Luke.

Luke thought for a minute and then agreed.

"I like that idea," he said. "I'll ask Miles to see if he can order one and have it delivered to the house. Great idea! Thanks!"

"Hey," Luke added. "I might have a couple of people with me for a few days when I come. How about you getting Pop prepared for that? He gets a little off when there is a change in his routine. If you want, call that Magnolia lady and have her send over a chef for a few days. I don't want you stuck cooking for a crowd," he told Addison.

"I don't mind," was her reply.

"Up to you," he said. I will be in early Saturday. They will get there on Monday. Just two more plus Miles. They leave on Thursday," he said, still very vague about who was coming.

"Can you get Maria to freshen up the two guest rooms? Maybe order a bunch of fresh flowers for one of them," he told her.

"Who's coming," Addison finally asked.

"Just a singer I've been working with. Her name is Barbie Jo. We are both performing at a 4th of July celebration and we're going to practice our duet. We haven't been able to connect very much with our tour dates. She's in Cincinnati now and I'm still in Philadelphia," Luke said.

"Hey how about your man, Danny Perez?" Luke asked.

"What?" said Addison, her voice ascending into a higher pitch. She had never told anyone there about her relationship with Danny.

"You know, the whole getting caught with two hookers and the steroids in his system stuff," Luke said. "You had to have heard about that. I bet he'll be back on the farm next week."

She had heard about Danny Perez. It was on the front page of STAR magazine that she saw at CVS when she and Pop went there to pick up some shaving supplies and a few other things. She bought the issue and as soon as they got back to the house, she called Maggie Grace who was ecstatic about the news.

"Couldn't have happened to a better low life," her friend said. "Go Karma, Go Karma" Maggie had said laughing, and then chanting, "Go Danny, Go Danny, Go to Hell Danny."

"I heard something about it," Addison said to Luke with a flat expression.

The conversation ended with Luke telling her he would call Pop around four, and that he was ready to come home for a few days.

Inside that same Star Magazine were photos of various pop stars and juicy bits of gossip and bavardage to smear their reputations. In the collage of photos of the various celebrities were three of Luke, all with a very pretty redhead named Barbie Jo Bentley. In one photo the two are walking in a park together, in the next they were at a restaurant. He was in a suit jacket, and she had a very low-cut dress on, and they appeared to be toasting each other with their wine glasses. In the third, she was wearing his favorite ball cap and a tee shirt that said "TAKEN" on the front.

This had irritated Addison so badly that she felt like crying. But why, she wondered. It wasn't like she and Luke were an item. There was no romance between them. She was just an employee hired to look after his grandfather. Yet she felt like they were close friends. They talked often on the phone. He told her how the tour was going. He laughed with her. They shared a lot, well almost a lot. He certainly didn't share anything about Barbie Jo.

"I've turned into an Internet stalker," Addison confessed to her best friend Maggie Grace when she called her that evening after Henry went to bed.

"Do you want me to pull you out of there? It might be for your own good," Maggie told her friend. "You're getting too attached, and I told you when you started that you just can't do that!"

"No, I want to stay. I really like it here. But, honestly, are you near a computer? Google her, she just doesn't look like anyone I think he would be with," Addison said.

The two women continued to talk on the phone, each bringing up pictures of Barbie Jo. In one she was dressed in a leopard print thong swimsuit that had a leash type collar, stretched out on her hands and knees with a jungle backdrop. In another she had on a sheer white tee-shirt, braless, while bottles of champagne were spewing out, soaking the shirt. In another she was dressed in an all-leather Highlander outfit, holding a sword, her red hair blazing in sunlight.

An article they read described her as a sultry R & B singer and compared her to Sara Gazarek, Lena Horne and Kate Ryan. Another article said it didn't matter what she sounded like, her looks alone were worth the cost of a ticket. Still another said she was like the three "R"s - Ready, Ripe and Raunchy."

Addison just could not believe that Luke was bringing this woman here, to meet Pop, and that she had to order fresh flowers for her bedroom. The rest of that week was pure torture, and even Henry could tell that something was amiss.

Miles was the first to get out of the car when it pulled up to the front door. He even smiled when Addison and Henry came out to meet them. Addison thought he looked exhausted. His ruddy complexion appeared to be pallid, and he looked like he had lost some weight. Luke came out next, full of life and smiles. He hugged Henry and said how glad he was to be home, and then without warning, his strong arms lifted Addison in the air and spun her around in a circle.

"What would I do without you?" he said to her when he returned her feet to the floor. This has been my best tour ever, and you know why?"

Addison shook her head no.

"Because I didn't worry one day about Pop and how he was getting along. That really took a lot of pressure off me." Luke said, and then turned his head towards Henry while still holding Addison in his arms. "We just love her, don't we Pop?" Luke said, finally releasing her.

Henry beamed and agreed. "Yes, we should definitely keep

her," Henry added.

Henry loved the golf cart that Luke gave him for Father's Day. He immediately jumped into the driver's seat and drove around the front yard. He had it on the driveway, up the small bank and through the mulch to the grass and did a few circles around some trees. His facial expression was priceless and left no doubt that Henry was excited.

Their guests arrived Monday afternoon. Henry had been a bit out of sorts at the idea of having to share his grandson with outsiders so soon after he got home. Out of sorts turned into pure contempt when Barbie Jo and her driver Geoffrey arrived.

"Oh Poppy," Barbie Jo exclaimed when she was introduced to Henry. "I have heard so much about you." She then gave him a quick kiss on his lips and exclaimed to everyone, "Oh, my Luke, he is just precious," the words sounding like something you would say about someone's Shih Tzu.

Henry quickly took the sleeve of his shirt and wiped his mouth with it. The red lipstick stained the sleeve which annoyed him greatly. He walked away and sat in his recliner.

"Lover," Barbie Jo said to Luke. "Where should Geoffrey put our things? Can your housekeeper help him with my bags?" she said referring to Addison.

That was the first time she acknowledged Addison's presence. Addison shot a look at Luke and then walked over to Henry.

"Hey Pop, how about a quick drive down to the barn?" Addison suggested.

Henry bounded from his chair and walked out the door towards the golf cart parked by the pool gate. He and Addison left. Henry did not say a word all the way to the barn.

"She looks like a two-bit whore," Addison heard Henry say to Raymond, not realizing that she could hear their conversation.

The two men walked further away from her when Travis arrived, Henry still in full animation while they talked. Henry had pointed to his mouth and then spit into the grass. Twenty minutes or so later, Addison and Henry were driving back to the house. Henry had the power on the golf cart at a crawl, obviously he was not in a hurry to get back.

Dinner that night was outside by the pool. Addison had made a variety of salads and baked some potatoes. Luke was grilling steaks and Miles was in charge of the outdoor bar. Miles was usually abstemious about alcohol and junk food, but today, Addison noticed he had downed three Coors Light beers with supper and took a huge piece of the chocolate cake she had made.

"I have the best idea," Barbie Jo exclaimed after dinner.

"I think that Geoffrey and Addie should have a night off. I think the two of them should go out for a fine dinner tomorrow night, have a few drinks and laughs, and I will stay here and make Luke one of my famous gourmet meals," Barbie Jo said smiling at everyone.

"No, that won't be necessary," Addison said, "Besides, I need to be here to help with Henry."

"Oh, don't worry, I think we can get Poppy off to bed just fine before we have our dinner," Barbie Jo stated.

She then looked at Luke, who while surprised by the idea, didn't seem to mind it.

"I think that would be fine, Addison," he said. "I think we can manage, what do you think Pop?" Luke asked, turning to his grandfather.

Henry was about to speak when Barbie Jo interrupted him.

"I think it would be great for Miles to have a night off too, don't you agree Luke?" Barbie Jo said flashing her big green eyes at Luke.

"I don't need anyone to make plans for me," Miles replied gruffly, throwing the ice cube tongs into the ice bucket and walking into the house.

"It's settled then. Geoffrey can leave with Addison about seven, that way she can take care of Pop's dinner and not have any worries so she can enjoy her night off." Barbie Jo said as she stood up from the lounge chair she had been occupying. She pulled out three $100 dollar bills from a small clutch she had been carrying.

"My idea, my treat," she said as she handed the bills to Geoffrey.

So much for a spontaneous idea, Addison thought to herself.

Geoffrey had not said a word but shot Addison a big smile and winked at her.

About one in the morning, Addison was awakened by the sound of someone turning her bedroom doorknob. She got out of bed, thinking that Henry needed her, only to find Geoffrey standing in her doorway.

"What do you want?" she said to him, slightly alarmed.

"I thought we might get to know each other a little better before our date tomorrow night," he said with a creepy smile on his face. His hand began caressing the door frame as he stared hungrily at Addison's slender figure outlined beneath her night gown.

"I don't think so," she replied, trying to shut her door.

He put his foot in, blocking the closing.

"Come on now, I got a couple things that could make us both feel really good," he said patting a small package he had in his shirt pocket and giving her a leering smile.

Just then another bedroom door opened. It was Miles, still fully dressed and looking keenly at Geoffrey.

"Is there a problem?" Miles asked.

Geoffrey released his hold on the door frame.

"Geoffrey got confused about which room he was staying in," Addison said, feeling relief that Miles had come out of his room.

Miles looked at the two of them with no expression on his face. He then walked over to Addison's door and pointed towards the room Geoffrey was supposed to be occupying.

Neither man said anything, Geoffrey put his hands up and then turned and walked to his bedroom. Addison let out a deep breath and Miles could tell she was somewhat shaken.

"You okay?" Miles asked Addison.

She nodded yes.

"Better lock your door tonight," he said and then he returned to his room.

# CHAPTER ELEVEN

The next day was excruciatingly long. Addison dreaded the evening and wanted to tell Luke about her encounter with Geoffrey from the night before. She decided not to. She knew that Miles knew, and if he felt Luke should, Miles would tell him.

Addison and Henry spent most of the morning at the barn. She was surprised when she saw Miles show up driving the CJ-7 Jeep Renegade that he used around town. He did not say anything to them, but she did see him talking with Travis, Raymond and Dale. She wished that Miles would come over to see Henry working with Elsie, the horse Henry had selected to groom that morning. Miles, however, after speaking with the men drove off without even acknowledging that she and Henry were there.

After lunch, Addison stayed in her bedroom while Henry took his usual nap. She felt awkward being with Luke and Barbie Jo as the two of them laughed and made various innuendos with each other.

"Be invisible," she kept reminding herself, remembering the warning that Maggie Grace had given her before she came to work for Luke and Henry.

After Henry's nap she went with him to the living room.

Luke and Barbie Jo had gone horseback riding. Miles was just coming down from the studio as Henry and Addison passed by him at the bottom of the stairs.

"They get any practice in?" Henry said to Miles, his face pinched up with a look of disgust.

"Yeah, right," Miles said as he continued to walk past the two of them.

Henry sat down in his favorite chair. He did not want to watch TV, or talk, or eat a snack. He just sat there. His arms folded across his chest, his face a bit distorted from his lips being pressed firmly together and his chin extending outward. An hour passed in silence. Addison picked up a crossword book that she kept in the drawer of the coffee table and tried to work on one of the puzzles. She had a hard time concentrating on the words and did not make much progress with it.

"A six-letter word for a poisonous snake," Addison said out loud.

"Does it begin with B?" Henry answered.

Addison frowned at him. "No, a "T," she replied.

"A Taipan," she heard Miles answer, without realizing that he had re-entered the room.

"They are fast moving and really deadly," he said.

Addison was impressed as she added the word to the puzzle, looking up to see Henry and Miles exchanging glances.

Luke and Barbie Jo joined Henry, Miles and Addison when they came in from their ride. Even after a long afternoon of trail rides and Luke's personal tour of the ranch, Barbie Jo looked like she had just stepped out of a fashion magazine. Her hair was perfect, and her make-up was impeccable.

She had changed into a fresh pair of blue jeans, adorned

with Swarovski rhinestones and beads that were strategically placed to bring the viewers' eyes up her legs to the bottom of her derriere. The back pockets had downward pointed crystal triangles that also helped to create the best illusion of her curves. She wore a tight fitting "cowgirl" shirt with the top two buttons open, exposing the crevice of her voluptuous breasts. With every turn of her head, her full locks of red hair danced in the air settling perfectly on her shoulders. Luke left for a few minutes to get his guest the tonic water she requested.

"If you're gonna make lamb chops tonight you better cook a couple extra. Jimmy will want to make a sandwich with them tomorrow for lunch," Henry said breaking the silence in the room.

"Oh Poppy, thanks for the hint. Does Luke love lamb chops? I know how to cook them really well," Barbie Jo answered as she got out of her seat and kneeled next to Henry.

"Yup, he loves them," Henry replied. "And if you're gonna cook Brussel Sprouts make sure you put plenty of butter, salt and pepper on them," he added, slowly rocking in his chair.

"What else does he like?" Barbie Jo asked Henry reaching out to hold his hand.

"Well let me think," Henry said. "He likes that Buluga caviar stuff, likes the way the little eggs explode in his mouth. Lots of Champagne too," Henry told her. "Oh yeah, he likes lots of rice. Brown rice and black beans. What he likes the most are brownies," Henry added after thinking for a few moments.

Addison and Miles gave each other a curious look. Addison had to keep from smiling because she knew everything that Henry had just said was a lie. He had told Barbie Jo everything that Luke hated to eat, except for the brownies.

Addison concluded that Henry added those knowing how much he liked to eat them and had assumed there would be some leftover.

Shortly after that, Barbie Jo and Geoffrey left to go to the grocery store. Barbie Jo made a big deal about how special the dinner was going to be and that she just had to go and pick up all the groceries personally.

Coyly, Barbie Jo said to Luke as she was leaving, "I think you will like the dessert I have planned the best."

Barbie Jo blew a kiss in Luke's direction as she left, and Henry sat, still rocking with a look of great satisfaction on his face.

# CHAPTER TWELVE

Henry didn't seem to have much of an appetite even though Addison had fixed Shepherd's Pie, one of his favorite meals for dinner. She generously layered the browned ground beef with peas and carrots and swirled mashed potatoes over the top. The casserole was baked in the oven until the butter she had dotted on top melted and lightly browned the tips of the potatoes. For dessert she had prepared a warm tapioca pudding with extra meringue that she gently folded into the boiled mixture when she took it off the stove.

She had been a bit frustrated trying to make Henry's dinner. Addison had to work around the bags of groceries that Barbie Jo had left on the counters and sort through the items that had been tossed and shoved into the refrigerator.

"Don't worry about putting Poppy to bed," Barbie Jo told her after Addison had cleared his supper dishes. "Luke and I can handle that," she added. "You better go get prettied up for your date. Have you got any nice clothes to wear?" Barbie Jo asked with an impudent tone.

An hour later, Addison emerged wearing a black and white Stella McCartney striped jumpsuit. The comments Barbie Jo had made infuriated her. To imply that she did not have suitable clothes or that she needed extra time to get "prettied up" cemented the dislike that Addison felt towards Barbie Jo. She had plenty of chic clothes to choose from but had not needed them for the relaxed lifestyle at the ranch. Years as a diplomat's daughter had allowed her many opportunities to dress elegantly and she had been to Fashion Week events that were held in New York City, London, Paris and Milan.

When selecting her attire for the evening, she decided that she was certainly not going to wear a dress when she was alone with Geoffrey. She felt the jumpsuit was provocative enough with the one shoulder top that exposed her right arm and tanned décolleté. Addison accessorized her outfit with four-inch black open toe heels and a matching fold over Louis Vuitton clutch. Her long hair was loose and flowed over her shoulders, and her bright red lipstick matched the color of her well pedicured toes. Addison had applied her make-up with the art and flare of a professional artist. The smoky eye shadows, black eyeliner and mascara made her deep blue eyes pop. She wore a David Yurman choker around her neck and coordinating John Hardy bracelets on her wrist.

Barbie Jo was speechless when she saw the transformation of the girl she had seen for the past two days, into this stylish young woman who looked like she could walk the red carpet at the Academy Awards. Even Luke had an expression of surprise on his face. He had always thought Addison was pretty, but tonight, she was a knockout!

Geoffrey was dressed in tight jeans with an open bright tangerine colored shirt and a white jacket. He had black shoes on, with no socks, and a wide gold chain around his neck. Geoffrey smiled at her with hungry eyes.

"Where are you heading," Luke finally asked after complimenting Addison so much that she blushed.

Barbie Jo was not happy with the attention Luke was showing towards Addison. At this point, Miles jumped into the conversation.

"I made a list of suggestions, and a few reservations, since Addie and Geoffrey don't really know the town too well," Miles said, handing the list to Addison.

"I thought they could start by having dinner at the Marsh House and then catch some music at Layla's down by the river on Broadway," he said.

"That sounds great," Luke said enthusiastically. "Both are two of my favorites," he added.

Addison left reluctantly. Geoffrey walked out with her, placing his hand on the small of her back and leading her towards the car. He opened the door and then dashed around the car to the driver's seat.

The car was a Chevy Corvette Stingray Convertible with Torch Red paint and a Z51 Performance Package. It had a grounds effect kit, a grille insert, and side mirror caps that were finished in carbon fibers. The wheel set measured 19 inches in the front and 20 inches in the rear with a five-spoke design and a performance pewter painted finish.

This car is perfect, Addison thought to herself. It reflects Barbie Jo's need for constant attention, and Geoffrey's need to feel like he's the big man on campus.

Trying to make small talk on their drive into Nashville, Addison asked Geoffrey how long he had been working for Barbie Jo.

"Long enough to know all of her secrets," was Geoffrey's

reply."

"Secrets?" Addison replied, genuinely curious.

"Oh, yeah," he said, exaggerating the words. "I could write a tell all book that would make your head spin."

"Really?" Addison said, trying not to sound too eager for the information.

"These," he said, patting his chest, "Fake." Geoffrey then made a hand motion like he was flipping his hair. "Extensions and fake color," he stated. Geoffrey then leaned over towards Addison and flashed a big smile. "Those," he said, "all capped. There is not a single part of her that has not been pinched, tucked, sucked or enhanced." Geoffrey said.

'Wow," was Addison's reply. "It all looks so natural."

"Top dollar baby, top dollar," Geoffrey said nodding his head. "But of course," he added, "she didn't have to pay for most of it."

"Sponsors?" Addison asked.

"Yeah, from the bank of *I'll Screw Anybody to get Ahead,*" he said, breaking out in a big laugh.

Addison was speechless. She could not believe what she was hearing, and she could not believe that Barbie Jo's employee would be talking this way about her. After a few moments of riding in silence, Geoffrey leaned over towards Addison and said,

"Looks like your dude's the next pigeon," he said to Addison.

"What do you mean?" she asked.

Geoffrey did not answer, he wanted Addison to give him a little more attention for the juicy tidbits he was telling her. She did not oblige.

"Barbie's an okay singer," Geoffrey said, "but she needs

to partner up with an "A" gamer if she is really going to get anywhere. She's got it planned out. Record a few duets, tour with him, turn up the heat, and who knows, find some scandal in it all that will boost her in the tabloids. She can get pretty damn crazy too, if things don't go her way. She gets that from her mother. Now she is one conniving bitch, Barbie Jo is a pussy cat compared to her," Geoffrey said with a tone mixed with confidence and arrogance.

"Aren't you worried about talking like this?" Addison said. "I had to sign a confidentiality agreement when I came on board."

Geoffrey laughed. "I got too much on her to worry about that," he said. "And besides," he continued, "she likes the service I provide, all the services," he said reaching out and stroking Addison's thigh.

"Stop that," Addison said sharply, pushing Geoffrey's hand off her leg.

He looked at her, and then returned his eyes to the road sulking. To show his irritation, he hit the gas pedal and brought the car up to 90 mph. Addison was scared, but she was not going to show it.

"A lot of cops around here," she said.

Reluctantly, he brought the speed back down to 50 mph.

When they arrived at the Marsh House for dinner there was a long line waiting to be seated. Thankfully, Miles had made a reservation and they were shown to their table as soon as they checked in with the hostess.

Addison caught a glimpse of a familiar face as they walked to the table. Travis was there with his wife. He gave her a quick nod, and Imani turned and smiled at her as she walked past.

Addison smiled to herself. She was surprised to see them but felt a sense of relief knowing they were there.

Travis and Imani were the most gorgeous couple she had ever met. Imani had been a finalist in the Miss Black Universe pageant and had just been promoted to a partner in the law firm that she worked for in Nashville. Next to Miles, Travis was the second most important member of Luke Johnson's entourage. The oversite of the Brentwood estate fell to Travis, although he liked to pretend that he was just a "good old boy" hired to help out with Henry. Tonight, Travis looked like he had just stepped off a GQ photo shoot.

More relaxed now, her naturally cheerful personality began to surface, and she had an enjoyable meal. The food was sensational, and she really was enjoying a dinner prepared by someone else and being waited on. Geoffrey thought he was winning her over and started to make some suggestive comments about her hair and figure, as he ordered more wine for the table. This did not impress Addison at all and made her long for the evening to end even sooner.

Geoffrey tried to impress Addison by leaving a big tip when dinner was over.

"Why not', Addison thought, it's not your money, she said to herself.

The valet brought the car up and Geoffrey gave the young man a $50 bill. He and Addison got in the car and he headed down towards the river. Geoffrey flew past *Layla's.* Addison asked if they were going to stop there. Geoffrey indicated that they were not, and said he thought they would head over to *The Stage on Broadway*, a popular place with live country music. Addison sat back in her car seat. A familiar looking CJ-7 pulled up next to their car and then drifted back behind them.

That can't be Miles, she thought to herself.

When Geoffrey pulled into *The Stage*, the CJ-7 did not stop. The two entered the bar. Geoffrey ogled the waitresses and some of the girls on the dance floor as they made their way to a table. Geoffrey quickly drank two shots of tequila while Addison sipped on her Ultra, declining his request to dance.

'I don't know what the hell I came out with you for," he told her. "You might be easy on the eyes, but you are no fun to be with. Do you think you're too good to be out with me?" he asked, greatly agitated. "You and me are the same baby, just the hired help," he said, leering at her. "Maybe you're getting some on the side, too," he added. "Or maybe the old's man getting off," Geoffrey added with a laugh.

Addison was disgusted. She thought about calling an UBER but knew he would only end back at the ranch with her regardless.

They were both surprised when Miles, Dale and Tim, another one of the ranch hands, came up to their table. Dale gave Geoffrey a friendly slap on the back and Miles acted like they were surprised to see them there.

"I thought you guys were going to Layla's," Miles said.

"I like this place better," Geoffrey said, still surprised to see them.

"Got some hot chicks here, don't you think?" Miles said, to Geoffrey, like he was talking to his best friend.

"They sure do," Jeffrey said with a grin.

"What are you drinking?" Dale asked, flagging down a waitress.

Geoffrey had two more shots and a large draft.

Miles leaned in closer to him and whispered, "How you making out with the nurse maid?" He asked, looking in Addison's direction.

Geiffrey snorted and shook his head.

"Check out those three girls over there," Miles said. "They've been looking at you all night."

Miles gave him a nudge with his elbow.

"Think you could handle all three of them?," he asked.

"Don't you worry about that," Geoffrey slurred. "I got my little blue pills right here," he said patting his front left trouser pocket.

"I've got a key here to a room at the Hampton, just in case I didn't make it back to the ranch tonight, know what I mean?" Miles said, holding the key up to Geoffrey. "Why don't you go ask one of them to dance? Maybe you'll need the key more than me."

Geoffrey gave Miles a big smile.

"You know, you're okay, you know, buddy," Geoffrey said to Miles, his words slurring.

The two men then turned and looked at Addison, who turned her head pretending that she had not heard any of the conversation.

"I'll take her back to the ranch; you go and have a good time," Miles said.

He then gave a quick look to Dale and Tim and the two of them pulled Geoffrey over to the girls and in a few minutes the six of them were dancing.

"You ready to leave?" Miles asked Addison.

"An hour ago," was her reply.

Miles stood up, waived to the waitress and gave her four $100 bills.

"Use that for their tab until it runs out, but make sure you save some tip money out of it," he said and then he and Addison started towards the door.

"What about the guys?" Addison asked.

"They will be heading back shortly. Ray might need some help at the barn," Miles answered.

# CHAPTER THIRTEEN

Luke sat with Henry, strumming his guitar and singing a bit while Barbie Jo was in the kitchen preparing dinner. She had told Luke their meal would be ready about eight thirty. After spending some time together, Luke walked Henry to his bedroom, helped him with his evening routine and tucked him into bed.

"We haven't done this in a while," Luke said reflectively as he pulled the light blanket up to his grandfather's chin.

"I miss it," Henry replied. "When are you coming home to stay for a while?" he asked.

"I start my summer tour Friday," Luke said. I'll be home for Labor Day, and then you get to go back to Virginia and spend some time with Aunt Helen." Luke reminded his grandfather.

Henry gave a slight smile and nodded.

"Is Addie going with me?" Henry asked.

"Maybe for a week, till you get settled in. Then she needs some time off to visit her family, don't you think?"

Henry looked disappointed, but softly said, "I guess so."

"I am thinking about having Barbie Jo join the band, and maybe go on the summer tour with me. What do you think about that?" Luke asked his grandfather.

"I don't think that is a good idea," was Henry's reply. "No sir, I think that would be a big mistake."

Henry then rolled over, unwilling to go any further with that conversation.

He did not give Luke the opportunity to tell him that Barbie Jo's manager would be coming the next day, and that he had instructed his agent to write up a contract for the tour dates.

Despite his best efforts to please Barbie Jo, Luke was not enjoying his dinner. He hated the smell of the food, and it was pretty obvious that despite her boasting, Barbie Jo did not know her way around the kitchen. He had enjoyed the tossed salad, but nothing else tempted him. He wasn't sure how to get around not hurting Barbie Jo's feelings when Henry appeared in the doorway.

"I think I need some help," Henry said.

Both Barbie Jo and Luke instantly saw the large wet stain on the front of Henry's pajama bottoms.

"I must have knocked over my glass of water," Henry said sheepishly. "My sheets are all wet too," he added.

Barbie Jo tried her best to give a big sympathetic smile to Henry.

"I've got this," Luke said, getting up from the dinner table.

"What happened Pop?" he was asking as he led his grandfather back to his bedroom.

I hate that old man, Barbie Jo said to herself. I hate him, and that Addison. I am getting rid of both of them as soon as the tour is over, she thought.

Shortly after Luke got Henry into dry pajama bottoms and changed the sheets on his bed, Raymond called up to the house.

"Looks like someone left a gate open and Gypsie got out. I

heard some coyotes earlier, so I am going to head out and look for her. I just wanted you to know," Raymond told Luke. "It might take me awhile. Travis, Dale and Tim have the night off, so I am a little shorthanded." He added.

"Damn," said Luke. "I'll be right down to help," he said to Raymond, holding his hands up and shrugging his shoulders as he looked at Barbie Jo.

"I am sorry, Sugar," Luke said when he hung up the phone. "This is a working ranch, and I have to help."

Barbie was mad. She tossed her napkin on the table and folded her arms pouting.

"And what am I supposed to do while you are running around chasing some stupid horse?" she asked angrily.

Luke had not heard that tone from her before.

"That stupid horse," Luke repeated, "I've got close to $40,000 invested in that horse and another $15,000 for breeding fees," Luke said, grabbing his hat and heading out the door.

Barbie Jo was furious. She knocked over the flowers that were on the table, and thought about throwing her plate at the wall, but she stopped herself. After spewing a long line of obscenities, she went to her room and grabbed the purse she had tossed on the dresser. Looking inside she pulled out a small plastic bag, similar to the one Geoffrey had in his pocket the night before. She poured herself a tall glass of wine from the wine chiller in her room and swallowed the pills.

"Well at least tonight won't be total lost," she said to herself as a wave of euphoria inched across her mind and body. She wondered what time Geoffrey would be back as she drifted off to sleep.

When Miles and Addison reached the ranch, they immediately saw the dishes left on the dining room table, along with the destroyed centerpiece, uneaten food and half full glasses. Addison walked past it and into the kitchen. She left out a low gasp when she opened the door. There were pots, pans, knives and multiple cooking utensils all over the counters and tabletop. Food had been left out, the garbage was overflowing, and the sink was full of dirty dishes.

Miles came up behind her.

"Remind you of anything?" he asked half laughing.

Addison gave him a quick smack on his arm and started walking towards the sink. He left the room and came back carrying an armful of dishes.

"I'll help," he said.

Addison stood there wearing the blue apron with little flowers she had retrieved from the pantry. She stared at Miles. This man, who had vexed her since her first day on the ranch, had turned into her savior over the last two nights. He had helped her when Geoffrey accosted her at her bedroom door and saved her again this evening from a night of misery with him. She knew that it was Miles that followed her to the bar and had orchestrated Travis, Dale and Tim to be there tonight to watch over her, and now he was offering to help clean up the pathetic mess that Barbie Jo had left. Maybe, just maybe, there was more to Miles than she had seen. There had to be a reason that Luke liked and depended on him so much. Was that the side of Miles she was finally seeing?

"Where do you think they are?" Addison asked, referring to Luke and Barbie Jo.

"I have a good idea that Luke is down at the barn," Miles

said with a grin. "I don't know, and frankly, I don't care, where she is," he added.

Addison smiled. "The enemy of my enemy is my friend," she recited to herself as the two walked over to the sink and Miles picked up a dish towel.

"You do look good in that apron," he said with a slight smile when they were done. "I think I'll go down to the barn for a while," he added.

About an hour later, Luke came through the door. He looked tired and wet. It had started to rain outside. He was surprised to see Addison at home.

"How did your date go?" Luke asked her.

"He left me for three hot chicks," she said.

"Left you?" Luke sounded alarmed. "How did you get home," he asked.

"Miles," was all she replied.

"Miles?" he repeated in disbelief. "He came down to the barn, and never said a word. This night just gets stranger and stranger."

"How about you?" she asked. "Did you have a good night?"

"Well, after Pop peed all over himself and his bed, and Gypsie decided to go for an evening stroll, and I got soaking wet looking for her, I guess you could say this wasn't one of my best evenings," Luke said.

"Barbie Jo?" quizzed Addison.

"Don't know," Luke replied flatly. I am guessing she wasn't tidying up the place when you got here."

Addison shook her head no.

"What about Gypsie?" Addison asked.

"Turns out she wasn't loose at all, just in a stall with one of the other horses. I don't know how Raymond missed that. We spent hours looking for her," Luke replied.

Addison smiled. I guess Miles kept a lot of things safe tonight, she thought to herself.

"Any chance there is any of that Shepard's Pie left?" Luke asked. "I'm starving."

"I'll have it ready by the time you get into something dry," Addison said getting up from her chair and heading for the kitchen.

# CHAPTER FOURTEEN

Geoffrey finally showed up around noon the next day looking very disheveled. He reeked of alcohol and his eyes were bloodshot. Addison could hear Barbie Jo lashing out at him and telling him to pull himself together.

Later in the day, Gloria Reynolds arrived at the ranch with Joe, a photographer Gloria brought to shoot Barbie Jo and Luke signing the contract for the summer tour. No doubt that photo would be "leaked" to the National Enquirer later that night with some sensational headline that suggested more than a business deal. Gloria had brought a bottle of champagne to toast the event with, the perfect tools for a suggestive photoshoot.

Barbie Jo's cell phone rang about fifteen minutes into the small chit chatting that was taking place. She checked the caller ID, and then excused herself to answer the phone.

"Oh my, it's my mama," Barbie Jo said getting up. "She depends on hearing from me every day," she added, smiling sweetly as she exited the room. "Probably wants to tell me about something she canned today…." Barbie Jo was saying, trying to add a southern accent to her native New Jersey dialect as her voice drifted out of earshot.

At about the same time, Luke's cell phone rang.

"Hey Chip," Luke said as he answered the call.

Chip was one of Luke's band members that had been at the house earlier that day so the band could practice with Barbie Jo. They were working on fitting her into some of the choruses and the score for a couple duets she would be singing with Luke.

Luke listened intently to his friend on the phone and then told the small group what Chip needed.

"Chip's been pulled over for speeding and needs his license. He says he took his wallet out of his back pocket today, but he is not sure if he left it in the studio when we were practicing or down at the barn before we all went riding. He needs someone to bring it down to the police station so he can pay his bail and get released."

Addison got up and motioned that she would check the studio and see if it was there.

"Turn the speaker on and let me know if you find it," Luke said as she was leaving the room.

"Chip," Luke said into the cell phone, "ask the officer if we find it, could we text him a picture of the license and pay the bail with a charge card over the phone."

A few moments later Chip replied that it had to be cash or a money order.

"Ok Buddy, just hold on and we will get right back to you." Luke said before hanging up the phone.

In the meantime, Miles was on his cell, calling down to the barn to have the guys look there.

Addison turned the lights and the speakers on when she entered the practice room. She walked down to the stage area and looked on the control panel but did not see anything. Pulling back a few of the stools, Addison dropped down to her knees to look under them. She heard the studio door fling open and was about to call out but stopped when she heard Barbie Jo's voice.

"You don't have to worry about that, I have him right where I want him." Barbie Jo's voice was confidently speaking into the phone.

'Yes, I have a plan," she continued, her voice starting to sound a bit annoyed with whomever she was speaking with."

"I plan to get pregnant," she said flatly.

"No, I am not crazy. I am not leaving here until that tiny Luke Johnson seed has been planted."

"Cute." she said, sounding annoyed.

"No, I am not the "hoe," she answered sarcastically, "I am the precious garden."

Addison was so taken aback by this conversation that she was frozen in her kneeling position, until she lost her balance and fell forward, her hand slapping the floor to catch herself.

"Who is that?" an angry voice called out.

"I'll call you back," Barbie Jo shouted into the phone as she walked briskly down to the console panel.

"You bitch," Barbie yelled at Addison. "Are you spying on me? What do you think you are doing?"

Addison slowly stood up, holding the wallet. She started to explain why she was there, and what she was doing, but Barbie Jo would not give her a moment to speak.

"You are not going to ruin this for me," Barbie Jo shouted sharply at Addison.

"I've seen the way you look at him. I know you want him," Barbie Jo continued. "But you can't have him! He's mine," Barbie Jo shouted at Addison. "You think we are hot on stage together?

Well let me tell you something Missy, we are even hotter off stage. He can't keep his hands off me." Barbie Jo was ranting.

"So, you and Jimmy are in a relationship?" Addison said, trying to placate her nemesis.

"Jimmy? Jimmy? Why the hell are you calling him Jimmy? His name is L-U-K-E, Luke!" Barbie Jo shouted back at her, as she spelled his name out loud.

"Pop calls him that." Addison said in a quiet tone.

"Pop, Pop, Pop! I am sick of that old man, and I am sick of you," Barbie Jo said her eyes glazed over and her voice full of venom.

"Jim…I mean Luke, loves his grandfather," Addison said softly.

"Well as soon as he finds out about our baby that old man is gone, they have nursing homes you know and once he is gone, you are out the door." Barbie Jo sneered moving extremely close to Addison, their faces just inches apart.

"Luke loves children," Addison said, trying to diffuse the situation.

"Yes, and he will love our baby," Barbie Jo said shifting her eyes off Addison for a moment as her mind fantasized about the family she envisioned.

Addison took that opportunity to quickly move out of the control area and skirted up the steps towards the door.

Barbie Jo followed her and grabbed Addison's arm.

"Don't think for a minute that you are going to spoil my plans," Barbie Jo said.

"Luke will never fall for this, or believe you," she replied pulling her arm away from Barbie Jo.

"Believe me?" Barbie Jo glared. "Anything you say, I will

deny. Who do you think he is going to believe? His partner, his lover," she said smirking at Addison, "or some two-bit housekeeper?"

Addison broke away from Barbie Jo's hold and exited the room. Barbie Jo was close behind. When they got back to the living room Barbie Jo was completely composed, gleaming with the bright smile she had used all day.

"Look who I found," Barbie Jo said smiling at everyone.

"Luke, you are so lucky to have her. I wish I could just steal her away from you," Barbie Jo said looking in Addison's direction.

Luke did not answer. Nobody answered. He walked across the room where the two women stood. He smiled at Addison, and gently brushed her cheek with his hand. Then, unexpectedly, he pulled her close and kissed her.

"I just can't keep my hands off of you," he said staring at Addison, still brushing her cheek.

Addison paused, and then nodding her head, she replied, "I know what you mean."

Addison could see Miles standing near them with Dale and Tim. She glanced at Barbie Jo, and then wrapped her arms around Luke's neck as they shared a deep passionate kiss.

If only this was real, Addison thought as she melted into Luke's strong arms. Dale and Tim came up behind Barbie Jo and locked their arms around her while she was distracted by Luke and Addison's embrace.

Gloria stood up trying to utter apologies and make excuses, to no one really listening, about the stress of the business. Joe was busy shooting pictures of everything he could, while Miles was steering them both towards the door. The contract had been ripped up and laid on the table. Pop was yelling, and Barbie Jo was screaming.

Travis was waiting out front with a car to take Gloria and Joe to their hotel. Dale and Tim were loading Barbie Jo, who was still screaming, into the car Geoffrey was driving. Luke stepped back and asked Addison if she was okay.

"Do you want to press charges for assault?" Luke asked her?"

"No, but she needs some serious help," Addison replied.

"I am getting a restraining order. She is done in this business. She's a real whack job," Luke said. "I should have seen that sooner. We were about to rush in, but you seemed to be handling it. I knew if you wanted us, you would have called for help. We could hear everything," Luke told her.

Addison sighed. "It was a bit tense," she said, and then with a smile, she held up Chip's wallet.

Luke chuckled, and said to Miles who had re-entered the room, "Tell Chip we have his license and tell him whatever the cost, we have his bail and ticket covered."

# CHAPTER FIFTEEN

At eleven the next morning, a red SUV drove up the long driveway. A nice-looking man parked the vehicle and came up to the door. Miles opened it and looked annoyed at not knowing who this stranger was, and why the security guard at the gate let him come up. The man extended his hand to Miles and introduced himself as Pastor Rich.

Addison came to the door and greeted the young Reverend warmly.

"What a nice surprise," she said. "Come on in," she added.

Miles looked at her, then him, and then her again as the minister entered the home.

"I was worried something was wrong when you and Henry didn't come to Seniors yesterday," Pastor Rich said as he entered.

"We had some out-of-town visitors," Addison replied.

"Look Pop," she said to Henry who was curious about who was at the door. "It's Pastor Rich, he came to see you," Addison exclaimed.

"Hello Mr. Lukens," the minister said, shaking Henry's hand when he approached him. "We were worried when you did not come to Seniors yesterday, so I thought I would check on you."

"We had an awful day here yesterday," Henry said shaking his head. "The Devil was here. We might have needed you to do an exorcism," he told the young preacher.

Pastor Rich had not expected that reply and looked at Addison with some alarm. She shrugged her shoulders.

"He can get confused when we have a lot of people around, and Luke's band and some others were here most of the day," she said trying to downplay Henry's comments.

A few moments later, Luke entered the room looking a little puzzled about who their guest was.

"Have you ever met Henry's grandson, Luke Johnson?" Addison asked Pastor Rich.

She took a few moments to introduce Luke and Miles to the minister reminding them about the senior's program that she took Henry to each Wednesday. Pastor Rich repeated his concern to Luke about Henry not attending the event the previous day, and that he had come just to check on him. Luke expressed his gratitude and asked a few questions about the program. He mentioned how happy he was that Henry had the opportunity to meet with people his own age and how much he thought his grandfather was enjoying the program.

"Is there anything you need for it?" Luke asked Pastor Rich. "I would be happy to help and sponsor something if you do."

"They need a new piano," Henry said. "Or at least they need to get the one they have tuned."

Luke looked at the Reverend who replied, "It is an old one. Someone from the church donated it after a family member," Pastor Rich paused here, he looked at Henry and then at Luke and added, "well you know, didn't need it anymore."

Luke knew exactly what he meant and volunteered to have a new one sent to the church.

"Get one of those self-playing pianos," Henry said. "Sometimes the regular girl can't come and the one that does, can't keep the tempo right."

Pastor Rich was embarrassed, and his face reddened a bit because he knew exactly who Henry was referring too, but he also knew how important it was to have people willing to volunteer for the church programs.

Luke smiled, "I'll look into that," he said.

Henry told everyone that he was ready for lunch and invited the minister to stay, who gladly accepted the invitation.

Luke, as always, was a gracious host. However, he felt himself becoming a little annoyed with the attention the minister was showering on Addison, and even more annoyed by how engaged she was with Pastor Rich's conversation. They referred to people and events that had taken place during the weekly gatherings that the others at the table could not relate to. They talked about how popular Henry was at the meetings and that he always had two or three of the ladies anxious to sit with him and monopolize his time.

"Thank goodness Pastor Rich is there," Addison said, "or I would have no one to talk to. Henry is too busy with his *lady friends,*" she said emphasizing the words and winking at Luke, "to spend any time with me."

Henry dismissed the comment as pure nonsense and asked if he could have another brownie.

As the luncheon continued, an interchange between Luke and Pastor Rich began to seem slightly competitive. Luke mentioned his playing varsity football in high school, Rich countered that he had been their team's quarterback. Luke said he had started college at Virginia Tech, before going into the service, Rich said he finished grad school and seminary at Duke. Luke talked about being on the road and traveling a great deal. Rich mentioned that he had worked on the church's Committee on Native American Ministries when he served in North Carolina and volunteered for a summer at the Red Bird Mission in the rural Appalachian Mountains in Kentucky. He had helped with their seniors' program which is why he started one at his current church. He had also spent two years working in a family counseling program at The Neighborhood Center in Utica, New York.

Unless asked a direct question, Miles sat back and just enjoyed what he considered was a pissing match between the minister and the country star. He looked at Addison who seemed to be oblivious to this, and at Henry, who was busy eating leftover brownies from Barbie Jo's dinner.

"I have never had the chance to thank you for all that you do for the church, and to tell you how much the youth enjoy the week here," Pastor Rich said to Luke.

Addison looked bewildered. Luke has never mentioned doing anything for the church, and what youth was Rich referring to she wondered?

"What youth?" she finally asked.

Pastor Rich waited for Luke to reply, but when he didn't, he tried to explain to Addison what he had referred to. Each summer the church hosted a camp for about fifteen middle school students from the inner-city. As part of the camp, they spend a few hours each day at the ranch riding horses and enjoying the fresh air. They end the week with a large BBQ and campfire.

"I didn't know anything about that, but it's my first

summer here," Addison said looking at Luke.

"Well Raymond takes care of all the details," Luke said. "We are just glad we can help with the program."

"It's a real blessing to these kids," Pastor Rich added.

"When does this take place," Addison asked.

"About the last week of July, right?" Luke said looking at Miles, who nodded an affirmation.

As Pastor Rich was preparing to leave, he turned to Addison and told her about the potluck picnic the church was planning for Sunday after the 11:00 service. The church provided hamburgers and hotdogs and the congregation was asked to bring salads, side dishes and desserts.

"It would be wonderful if you and Henry could come," he said, smiling at Addison.

He then quickly added that it would be great if Luke and Miles attended as well. They both declined and Henry said he had no time for picnics, so he did not think he or Addie would be there.

"Miss Polly and Miss Jane will be very disappointed," Pastor Rich replied to Henry, and then added, "I will be too," when his glance returned to Addison.

Addison blushed and said she would talk more about it with Henry.

Luke folded his arms and stiffened a bit as he watched the minister talk privately with Addison who had walked Pastor Rich to his car. Miles, who was standing on the porch next to Luke grinned and smiled as he watched Luke's reaction.

In a low voice Miles said to Luke, "I guess it wasn't Geoffrey we had to worry about," as he gave Luke a pat on the back and headed into the house.

"Hey Pop," Miles said, "got any of those brownies left?"

# CHAPTER SIXTEEN

Luke, Miles and the band headed out to make their Friday night concert stop. That weekend, Addison and Henry drove the golf cart down to the small lake to go fishing, picked some of the ripe tomatoes and cucumbers from their garden and watched a few episodes of "Airwolf" another TV show from the eighties that Henry had on DVD.

They did not go to the church service on Sunday, but Henry did agree to go to the picnic. Travis was home with his family, so Raymond drove them, and stayed for the fellowship as well. Raymond even stepped up and volunteered to help with the grilling. Pastor Rich was very glad to have them there and sat next to Addison for the luncheon.

On Tuesday, while Henry and Addison were brushing Elsie, Dale came over with a copy of US Magazine. Barbie Jo's picture was on the front page with the caption, "Engagement Broken!"

Addison flipped to the inside where a picture of Barbie Jo in tears appeared along with a picture of Luke passionately kissing another woman. The woman's face could not be made out, but it was certainly clear to Addison and everyone at the ranch that it was her.

The article claimed, based on information provided by a "close family friend," that the secret engagement of Barbie Jo to country singer Luke Johnson was called off when Barbie Jo caught him cheating on her with the unidentified woman.

The story went on to say that Barbie Jo was forced to cancel the summer tour she had planned with Luke because she couldn't face working with someone she could not trust.

Everyone at the ranch knew that Barbie Jo was actually at a rehab center in Canada recovering from a mental breakdown brought about by too much alcohol and too many pills.

The tabloid article described how devastated and betrayed Barbie Jo was. According to the source, Barbie Jo and Luke had talked many times about starting a family, but that now, Barbie Jo realized that Luke could not be trusted on the road. What hurts the most, the article stated, was how close she had become to Luke's family, especially his grandfather, and how broken-hearted she was to no longer be able to spend time with that dear old gentleman. Due to her heartache, Barbie Jo, even though she knew how disappointed her fans would be, was going to take the summer off to try to pull through this horrific event.

The unidentified source asked everyone to pray for Barbie Jo. It ended by saying that though deeply hurt, she forgave Luke and that she understands there are some women that will do anything to get in the way of someone's happiness. It ended with a quote from Barbie Jo asking everyone to pray that the unnamed woman would turn from her sinful ways.

Addison was furious when she read that. Dale and Raymond were chuckling, and Henry asked her what was wrong. She debated about saying anything to him, but her frustration took the better of her and she showed him the pictures and the article. Henry didn't read it, but he did look at the pictures.

After a few moments, Henry said, "Well that's a real nice picture of you and Jimmy. I'd like to see some more of those."

This caused Dale and Raymond to burst out laughing so wholeheartedly that Addison threw the magazine down and stomped off walking towards the house. About a quarter mile into her trek, Henry caught up to her with his golf cart and waited for her to climb back in.

In a voice that reflected clear mindedness, he told her not to let the article upset her. Everyone that mattered knew the truth, and trash like that comes with the territory. It wasn't the first lie ever published about Jimmy, and it wasn't going to be the last. Addison did not know why, but she could not help but cry. Henry wrapped his arms around her and gently patted her back.

"It will all be okay," he said gently.

When Danny had broken Addison's heart, she knew the pain that comes with betrayal. She never wanted to feel that way again, and she never wanted to be someone that would make another person feel that way either. That article implied that she had. She was hurt, and she was angry. What if her parents saw that, or Pastor Rich? Would they recognize her from the photo? Would they believe those lies? There were very few people she had ever totally disliked in her life, but Barbie Jo Bentley was one of them.

"Let's go out for supper," Henry said when they reached the house, hoping it would lighten Addison's mood.

"We can get Ray, Travis, Tim, anybody that wants to come, and go out and get a pizza," Henry suggested.

It was the perfect remedy that Addison needed. The

entire gang headed over to Sal's Family Pizza. The guys pushed together two of the wooden tables and ordered five different huge "Godfather" size pizzas that the restaurant was famous for. The toppings were fresh and plentiful, and everyone enjoyed the evening.

Addison loved the stories the fellows were sharing about life on the ranch, things they had done with Henry and Luke and a few even mentioned tricks they had played on Miles, just to get a laugh. Addison loved this big extended family and was thankful to be part of it.

Luke had called Henry, like he usually did in the afternoon. It bothered his grandson to hear how upset Addison had been by the magazine article. Henry relayed what he had told Addison, including his comment about wanting to have more pictures of her and Luke. Luke laughed. He was glad that his grandfather had suggested the pizza party.

When Henry and Addison got back to the house, a huge bouquet of red roses was waiting for her. The note was a message from Luke, expressing his sorrow about the article upsetting her. He ended it was a PS, "I liked our picture too."

After Henry went to bed, she poured herself a glass of Riesling, re-read the note as she admired the flowers, and called her best friend to talk over the events of the day.

"I think you left that part out," Magnolia was saying to her friend.

"What part?" Addison asked.

"The part where he is dreamingly kissing you that is now posted all over the magazine and the internet. You told me the two of you distracted the girl, you did not say that this was how you did it." Maggie said in a teasing voice.

Both women laughed. They talked for a full hour, catching up on the simple, mundane things of everyday life that only best friends would be interested in. When they finished, Addison opened her computer and wrote a long e-mail to her parents. She told them in full detail what she had been doing and how much she was enjoying her time in Tennessee.

# CHAPTER SEVENTEEN

Luke, Miles and the band were back on the road for the 4th of July celebration and his holiday performance at the Capital in Washington, DC. Luke had some other tour dates, and he was working on a project in Los Angeles. She knew they would be back before the July concert at the Ryman Auditorium at the end of the month. Luke had also said that he wanted to be there for the final night that the youth, from the inner-city program that helps and supports teens that needed positive mentoring and role models, would be at the ranch.

Despite daily calls, Addison could tell how much Henry missed his grandson. She missed him too. She even started to slightly miss a dose of Miles' daily sarcasm. The weather had turned hotter. The heat caused Henry to tire more easily and rest for longer periods of time. In the late mornings when Pop took his nap, Addison used the time to swim laps in the pool behind the house and sunbathe while doing yoga and stretching exercises.

She was unaware of the car that had driven up to the house and the three passengers that had disembarked.

Luke, Miles and Antonio were weaving their way through the house towards the kitchen. Antonio was the top selling country singer in Brazil. He and Luke had been working in LA cutting a couple of duets. They stumbled on Pop, who was perched on a chair in the kitchen, looking out the window with a pair of binoculars.

Luke's unexpected entrance into the kitchen startled his grandfather causing him to lose his balance. Luke was able to steady Henry and Antonio was quick enough to grab the binoculars that were falling from the old man's hands. Henry fiddled with his shirt and turned his attention to everything, except towards the window he had been looking out of. Antonio quickly took up the post Henry had left vacant. Miles, with his usual condescending tone asked Henry if he was bird watching, and then laughed at the thought, like it was a great joke.

Antonio, who quickly had focused on Addison doing yoga stretches in her bikini, let out a small whistle, and said, "Oh Pop, I like the birds you watch."

"What are you doing?" Luke asked his grandfather.

"I am just checking on Addie to make sure she is okay; she should not go swimming by herself you know," Henry said, trying to sound convincing.

"Addie?" Antonio said. "That is Addie?" He said again in astonishment.

Antonio put down the binoculars and continued saying to his friend, "This is the Addie you would not shut up about for the last two weeks? The Addie you said was so sweet and could cook and reminded you of your grandmother?" Antonio's tone was one of disbelief.

"I thought she was some little old lady. If this one

reminds you of your grandmother, then Henry, you were indeed a lucky man." Antonio said stretching out a high five hand to Henry who ignored him.

Luke walked over and grabbed the binoculars from Antonio and peered through them. For a moment he stood there in silence and then put them down on the counter.

"Pop, what do you think you are doing?" Luke asked. "Does she know you are in here spying on her?"

Henry hung his head down and said "no" like a young boy caught looking at his first Playboy. Luke looked disappointedly at him and headed for the door, calling Addison's name to let her know they were coming out.

As they were leaving the room, Henry called after them, "I ain't dead yet!"

Hearing the words, Antonio could not control a generous laugh as he and Miles followed Luke out to the pool.

Seeing them approach, Addison quickly pulled a cover-up over her suit and stood to greet them.

"I didn't know you were coming today," she said, somewhat embarrassed that her boss and these other gentlemen had found her at the pool.

"I was ready to come home," is all Luke was able to say, before Antonio pushed himself forward lifting Addison's hand and softly kissing it.

Luke, looking annoyed at his friend, introduced him to Addison. She smiled and then said that she better go in and check on Henry. Antonio stopped her, assuring her that Henry was fine, and that it was he that directed the three men to find her at the pool. Kissing her hand once again, he began to say something to her in Portuguese.

Luke rolled his eyes. He had seen Antonio capture the attention of many of the LA starlets by uttering a few words with his smooth tenor voice, only to later see them leave Antonio's hotel room.

Addison's reaction therefore took him wholly by surprise. Instead of the normal giggles he was accustomed to hearing, Addison recoiled her hand and her facial expression turned to anger and disgust. With no warning, she drew her hand and slapped Antonio across the face.

"Addie!" Luke yelled at the same time Miles shouted, "Are you out of your mind?"

Without looking at any of the men, she marched into the house. Luke turned to Antonio and started to apologize for her actions. Antonio held up his hand saying,

"No, No. Do not be angry. I probably deserved that. You did not tell me she spoke Portuguese."

"I didn't know," Luke began, "Hey what did you say to her anyway? I have never seen her mad about anything."

Addison walked into the house, right past Henry without saying a word, and up to her bedroom. By the time she had changed, all four men were standing, still bewildered, in the kitchen. When she reappeared, she stared at them for a moment, and then in a voice she tried to keep at a calm and even level, offered an apology to Luke's guest.

"No need," he repeated, "it is I who should apologize," Antonio replied. "Most Americans I meet do not speak Portuguese, most don't speak anything but English, and some do that rather poorly too."

Addison looked at Antonio and then at the other three men.

"In addition to English, I speak four languages fluently," Addison stated, trying to remain calm. "German, French, Spanish, and Italian. I know some Russian, Mandarin Chinese, and Portuguese," Addison continued. I have a master's degree with a double major in German and Spanish Literature and a Doctorate in Linguistics.

The four men stood there, no one knowing what to say or do.

"I wasn't planning on five for dinner tonight, so would anyone object if I ordered take out," she said in a tone that implied that it was a statement, not a question.

The men, still speechless, all shook their heads indicating that they would not mind at all.

"Or" she continued, "I can run to the market and get some steaks for the grill. I will let you know what I decide," she told them as she walked back out of the kitchen. She did not wait for a comment or reply from the men who were at a loss as to what surprised them more. Addison's assertiveness or the fact that she had a PHD.

Steaks grilled by Luke had been decided upon for dinner. The men insisted that they would take care of all the details. Miles went to the market and picked up five large filet mignon steaks along with fresh asparagus, corn on the cob and large potatoes for baking. He and Antonio manned the kitchen to prepare the vegetables. Pop had suggested a strawberry topped cheesecake for dessert, which Luke drove to the bakery and picked up.

They decided to eat on the patio and Henry set the table. Antonio escorted Addison to her chair where he had placed a long white box tied with a red ribbon. Inside were two dozen long stem roses and a written apology. He also presented her with a large box of Godiva chocolates as he repeated his pleas for her forgiveness and his most sincere apology for being so rude that afternoon. He never told Luke or Miles what he had said. Henry asked her at least twice if she planned on opening the box of candy that evening.

Addison could not keep up her pretense of being hurt and angry. After telling Antonio that she hoped he had learned his lesson and thanking everyone for the work they put into the dinner, an enjoyable evening was had by all.

Luke broached the topic of Addison's academic credentials.

"I can't believe you have a PHD," he said to Addison.

"Why, don't you think I am smart enough?" she said, pretending to be affronted.

"No, No," was Luke's quick reply. "I just mean," he fumbled for the words, "what is someone with a PHD doing working...," he did not know how to finish the sentence.

"It's Magnolia's," Addison said. "That company is very particular about who they hire."

That comment made Miles choke on the glass of beer he had just taken a gulp of.

"Do you really speak all those languages?" Henry asked? "Can you teach me how to swear in a few of them?"

Everyone laughed when he asked that.

In French, Addison said, "Je pense que vous êtes tous merveilleux." She followed that with German, "Ich denke, du bist alle wunderbar," and in Russian, "Я думаю, вы все замечательные." Looking at Antonio she added in Portuguese, "Eu acho que vocês são todos maravilhosos."

"What does all that mean?" Henry asked.

Addison looked at Antonio and asked him if he cared to translate. He smiled, look at the men in the jovial group and said, "She thinks you are all wonderful."

Addison nodded her head and added, "and that is true in any language."

Luke, Miles and Antonio had returned in time to participate in the last night of the youth program. The nine boys and six girls enjoyed a wonderful week. After daily activities at the church in the morning, they spent the afternoons at the ranch.

On Wednesday of that week, they had helped with the seniors' program by cooking and serving the meal. They enjoyed interacting with the older men and women. At the ranch, they swam and fished in the lake. They learned how to saddle and brush and fed the horses they rode each afternoon.

For the final afternoon and evening of the program, Raymond had organized an end of the week rodeo where the youth rode horses around large barrels, demonstrated how to put on and take off a saddle, and did a team relay race, passing a red bandana flag from one rider to the next. At the end, Luke awarded blue ribbons and gave each participant an IPAD fully loaded with games, music and educational apps. The kids loved it. He also told them, that he knew they were capible of doing good work in school, and if they finished high school and applied to college or a career school, that he guarnateed scholarship help would be available for them.

Henry and Addison came down to the field to watch the rodeo and stayed for the campfire as well. Pastor Rich was there, and he sat with them. Raymond had used Magnolia to arrange for a caterer to prepare a large dinner that included fried chicken, BBQ beef ribs, pork tenderloins, fruit, vegetable and pasta salads, and a large assortment of desserts for the youth, church volunteers that had helped that week, and for all the ranch staff.

Both Luke and Antonio performed songs and answered questions about life on the road as performers. The kids seemed to have a great time. Pastor Rich led the group in prayer before the youth loaded the bus to go back to the hotel that they had stayed in for the week. Addison did not know it, but Luke paid all the expenses for the outreach program for the entire week, including the housing. When the kids were gone, Antonio reflected on how much he truly enjoyed the event.

At breakfast the next morning, Antonio recalled his participation in a program called *Shade and Fresh Water* when he was a young boy in Brazil. He said the program helped him to make some positive life choices and helped him develop some leadership skills. He shared that back then, his father earned less than $3.00 a day and that he had to support his wife and eight children on that little income.

"Shade and Fresh Water," Addison said. "I know that program," she stated. "It's a missionary program, right?" she asked, not really addressing the question to anyone.

"Yes," replied Antonio.

Addison smiled, it was one of the programs she had spent a summer at with her mother many years earlier, although she did not share that with her friends. She wondered if Antonio had been one of the boys about her age that she had spent time with. There had been something familiar about his big smile and jovial laugh that she could not quite place.

The Ryman Auditorium concert was the next night,

and Addison and Henry attended. She loved the concert, and she loved watching Luke perform. Antonio also performed and he and Luke did three of the songs from the soundtrack that the two men had been working on in LA.

At the end of his visit, when Miles left to take Antonio to the airport, the awkwardness and disdain that Addison had felt towards Antonio when they first met had vanished. When he gave up his lady's man persona and desire to appear macho to Luke and Miles, Antonio was actually a very nice and funny man. They all parted as good friends.

# CHAPTER EIGHTEEN

The rain danced across the roof like a soft melody. Addison closed the patio door after taking a deep breath to enjoy the vanilla scented fragrance of the sweet autumn clematis that grew along the privacy fence. It looked like there were a thousand small pure white flowers drinking in the cool mist as the water trickled down the glass panes.

This was one of her favorite spots. It was intimate. Offset from the remainder of the massive living room, it was a haven for quiet conversation and meditation. Plush cushioned seating surrounded the Tuscan stone circular fire pit.

The large glass doors opened to a private patio where cushioned wicker lounge chairs invited repose. To the left of the glass doors was a steaming hot tub. Near that was a cozy covered bar and grill area. She reflected on how much she enjoyed the quiet dinners she had shared with Henry, Luke and Miles on the patio during the summer.

Waterproof solar LED lights illuminated the privacy fence and were carefully placed along the walkways and in the well-manicured shrubbery and ground cover. At the far end, were French doors that provided access into Luke's bedroom suite. Many times, when he could not sleep, Luke would come out and soak in the steaming water while enjoying the brilliant stars above. He said once that he had written his hit song, "On a Starry Night" while relaxing in the hot tub.

It was one of those rare evenings when only Luke, Pop and Addison were at home. Miles and some of the ranch hands had gone into town to hit a few spots and drink way too much, she conjected. Pop had gone to bed early. She kicked off her shoes and curled up on the white sofa watching the fire gently flicker.

"What are you thinking about?"

She heard Luke's voice call to her from the living room doorway.

Addison thought for a moment. "The graham crackers, Hershey chocolate bars and marshmallows sitting in the kitchen, and how feasible it would be sit here, and make s'mores," she replied as he walked closer.

"Hey, count me in," Luke said sitting down next to her.

"One problem.... not sure what to use to roast the marshmallows," she replied.

"I've got it covered," Luke said. "You go get the other stuff."

When she returned from the kitchen juggling the ingredients on a tray, she found Luke warming his hands by the fire. His hair was wet and there was a puddle of water by one of the glass doors. He held up a two-pronged grilling fork that he had secured from the outside bar.

"That rain is colder than you think," he said with a twinkle in his eye.

Addison laughed and handed him the paper towels that she had brought from the kitchen. He promptly used one to wipe his face and hands, and another to whisk through his hair.

"I guess it is coming down a little harder than you thought

too," she said smiling at him. They both laughed.

"Gimme those marshmallows," he said pretending to poke her with the grilling fork. Moments later they were each biting into the gooey treat.

"You know what this need," he said to Addison with his mouth half full of graham crackers.

"What," she replied.

"A cold beer," he said.

"A cold beer?" Addison repeated, bursting out laughing. "A cold beer with s'mores?"

"Yes," he said nodding his head.

She looked at him for a moment, and then giggling said, "sounds perfect!"

Luke was up in a flash and heading towards the kitchen.

"Bring napkins," she yelled after him.

He stopped for a moment and with a joking tone said, "Bring napkins? What do you think I am?"

"Perfect," she replied.

"What?" He said, stopping for a moment.

"Oh God," she thought. "When am I ever going to learn to think before I speak and not say things out loud," she said to herself.

She did think he was perfect. Perfect in every way. Perfect looks, perfect sense of humor, perfect strong arms, perfect blue eyes, perfect voice, he even smelled perfect.

"Did you say I am perfect?" Luke asked again.

"I said a cold beer would be perfect, napkins would be perfect, and you are perfectly wonderful to go and get them," she said back to him trying to laugh so it would lighten the moment.

"I'm perfect. Addison Albright thinks I'm perfect." Luke

said teasingly as he disappeared down the hall.

A few moments later he came back with a small cooler filled with ice and six beers. He also had a roll of paper towels.

"Are we expecting company?" Addison asked, laughing as he reached down into the cooler and brought up a cold Coors Light for her.

He held up one finger, as if to say "wait" and then brought out of the cooler a red solo cup. Addison cracked up laughing. He tore off a paper towel from the roll, handed it to her, and then opened the beer and poured it into the cup.

"Only the best for you my dear," he said handing the cup and towel to her. He then began to sing,

*"Red solo cup*
*I fill you up*
*Let's have a party*
*Let's have a party"*

Addison could not stop laughing.

"I think you are out of luck with that one," she said. "Toby beat you to it."

"Damn," Luke said, trying to look serious, "I can never catch a break."

He reached for a beer from the cooler, popped the top and took a big swallow.

"Are you ready for another?" he asked Addison,

"Beer?" She said holding up her full cup.

"No woman. Another s'more," he said. "You are falling behind. You're not trying to keep all that chocolate for yourself, are you?" he teased as he loaded two more marshmallows onto the grilling fork.

Later, as the two sat in quiet contentment staring at the flame, Luke asked, "Addison, what are you doing here?"

"What?" she said, taken aback by the question, and feeling insecure about why it was asked, and what the meaning was for it.

"What are you doing here?" he repeated as he turned and stared at her. "You're smart, you are funny, you are hands down gorgeous. What are you doing working as a domestic taking care of an old man?"

Addison blushed and felt a little nervous about her answer. "Truth is, I was only supposed to be here two or three days," she said in a soft serious voice.

"Two or three days? I don't understand." Luke said looking intently at her.

"Maggie Grace is my best friend from college. I showed up on her door with the worse broken heart ever. I just wanted to hide from the world."

She then went on to explain what had happened in Maggie Grace's office.

"She was about to send over a permanent replacement when Miles called her and said I was working out just fine, and that I was perfect for the job. So, she asked me if I wanted to stay longer, and of course I told her I would. Maggie Grace said he raved about me, which floored me because I thought Miles hated me."

"Miles is Miles," Luke said, shaking his head and trying not to grin. "But why did you stay?"

"I felt safe here," she said slowly. "Pop is amazing, and, well, I really love him. You're pretty amazing too," she added shyly. "You made me feel welcomed, and you did not treat me like a servant, and let's face it, you pay really well," she said exaggerating the word really. "A lot more than my last job."

"So, who was the guy...what did he do...do you still have feelings for him?" Luke asked hesitantly.

"Doesn't matter, cheated on me, and God no," she answered.

"How serious was it?" Luke asked.

"We dated all through college. Then he got a great career break. I had the engagement ring, dress bought, hall booked," was her reply. "I had even quit my job because his job took him on the road a great deal, and he wanted me to travel with him. We also thought about trying to start a family right away."

"Wow," was all that Luke could say.

"He did send a check to my folks for the cost of the dress and the deposit on the hall. He even told me to keep the ring."

Luke sat shaking his head. "I'd like to meet that guy. After I punch him in the face, you know, for what he did, I'd tell him he is a fool, and thank him for making a way for you to be here."

Addison smiled and leaned back into the soft cushions, her head looking up at the ceiling. They sat in silence for a few moments.

"So, Miles said I was perfect for the job...I just don't get him. I can't figure him out," she said turning her head towards Luke.

"Well, I guess since Pop did not bite you..." Luke said with a slight laugh.

After a few moments, Luke said, "Miles and I served in the Army together. We got into a sticky situation, and, well I guess you can say I kinda saved his life."

"You got a medal for saving someone...didn't you? So, it was Miles?"

"Yes," Luke replied, "and later when my first record went platinum, the Press made a big deal about it. Miles never wanted me to say his name to them. Anyway, after we got out, Miles just kind of followed me home. He said he owed me everything and that he would do anything for me."

Addison sat quietly and nodded her head.

"That was before I started my career. We were still kids. Still living on the farm in Virginia. Miles just kinda moved in with me, Pop and my grandmother."

"Where was he from? What about his family?" she asked.

"Miles had a crappy life. That is why he joined the Army. He grew up in foster homes, and some of them were not very nice. That's why we started the kid's outreach program here in the summer. Miles doesn't have any family that we know of. His grandmother was part of the Lumbee Indian Tribe. He was born in Pembroke, North Carolina. Miles doesn't know where his father was from or how he met his mother. He doesn't think they were ever married. When he moved in with us, he really took a liking to my grandmother. She was amazing! You would have loved her. We really miss her," Luke said with a mix of joy and sorrow in his voice.

"You know when you first started here, and you wanted that apron?" Luke said.

"Yes," Addison answered. "Miles gave it to me a few days later."

"Well, what you don't know is that my grandmother always wore a blue apron with little white flowers. So, when Pop said you needed one, and he wanted it like that, Miles could tell that Pop liked you. He personally went into town to the fabric store and bought the closest looking fabric to what she had, and then he took it to the company that makes my stage outfits and had them sew it just like hers," Luke told her.

"You are kidding me!" Addison said in astonishment, sitting up in her seat.

Luke grinned widely and shook his head no. "I swear it," he said. "That is a $700 custom made apron by one of the most exclusive designers in Nashville. Think about that the next time you are wiping your wet hands on it." He started laughing at that thought, and Addison smacked his arm and told him to stop it.

They sat again in silence for a few moments while Addison replayed the conversation in her head.

"I am going to have to treat that man a little nicer," she said. "I might even bake him something tomorrow."

"Well don't tell him I said any of this," Luke cautioned. "He didn't have much kindness growing up, and he doesn't always know how to accept it."

"So, Johnson. Why did you pick the name Johnson? I understand the Luke part, from Lukens, right? But where did Johnson come from?" Addison asked.

Luke nodded his head to acknowledge her question. "My dad's name was John, and I am John's son. So, Johnson."

"What happened to your dad?" she asked quietly. That's a picture of him with your grandparents in Pop's room, right?

"He enlisted. Died in the service. He was only nineteen." Luke said quietly.

"Sorry" she said, reaching over and touching his hand. "What about your mother?" she asked.

Luke took a deep breath and then said, "My mother. Now

that is a story," Luke said shaking his head.

He thought a moment about whether he wanted to share this story with her as he leaned his head back on the couch looking up at the ceiling.

"She was seventeen and my dad had just turned eighteen when he enlisted. He didn't know it, but he got her pregnant right before he left. When he found out, he vowed that he loved her, and he was going to marry her as soon as he could get home, but he never made it back."

"Well," Luke continued, "my mother's mother, my other grandmother, was madder than a hornet. From what I understand, she came over to the house, calling my father every name in the book, saying he ruined her daughter's life. Just every nasty thing you can think of, and all this within two weeks of Pop and Gram learning that their only child had died." Luke told her.

"That is horrible," Addison said softly.

"Well Tina, my mother, and her mother, Rhonda, told my grandparents that Tina was going to get an abortion. That she did not want to have anything to do with a baby, that she was not going to be saddled down with a kid and ruin her chances of marrying good. That broke Gram's heart. The thought of losing John and his baby," Luke added.

"I can't believe how cruel they were," whispered Addison, her eyes filling up with tears.

"So, Pop went and met with Rhonda. Seems that Tina was in her 4th month and, lucky for me, no one would do an abortion that far along back then. Pop worked out a deal with her. He had to mortgage his farm to do it," Luke said hesitantly.

"A deal?" Addison said in puzzlement.

"My great-aunt Helen told me all this once, Pop and Gram would never talk about it," Luke said.

"Rhonda did not want anyone to know that Tina was pregnant. She got Pop to agree to pay for an apartment for her and Tina to move to in Richmond and all their living expenses until the baby was born. They didn't have insurance, so Pop had to pay all medical expenses for the delivery. She also said that more than anything else, Tina wanted to go to college. Rhonda got Pop to agree to pay for the full four years of college including room and board. He was to give her and Tina the money for college up front, so that he could not change his mind once the baby was born. Like I said, he had to mortgage his farm to do that, but he did it," Luke said in hushed tones.

"Did I mention that Tina was the 4th generation of unwed mothers in her family, and the first to graduate high school?" Luke asked shaking his head.

"Anyway, Pop had a good head on his shoulders. He got a lawyer so that he and Gram could legally adopt me. Tina turned eighteen about a month before I was born. The lawyer had both her and Rhonda sign away any parental or family rights. They also signed a nondisclosure contract regarding the money Tina was getting. If they ever claimed that they knew anything about the baby Henry and Alice were adopting, that they both had to pay back the money with interest," Luke told her.

"I can't believe any mother would basically sell her baby. What happened to her, did you ever see her again?" asked Addison.

"Tina enrolled in one semester at the community college in Roanoke and flunked out. The last anyone saw of her or Rhonda, they were driving a flashy red convertible out of town with a small UHAUL behind it," Luke said shaking his head, his lips tightly pressed together.

"I never heard anything about them after that until I got my first Grammy Award. Rhonda died some time ago, and Tina showed up to tell me she was my long-lost mother and how she had spent her life searching for me," he said.

"She claimed that Pop and her mother had done everything behind her back and that Pop stole me from her. She wanted us to be a family again." Luke snorted here and his face started turning red.

"She said she wanted to move to Nashville to be closer to me, and could I give her $3,000 to help with the moving expenses? When I refused, she "sold" her story to the tabloids. They tried contacting us to confirm the story. Gram was really sick with cancer, and honestly, I think the stress of all that is what finally did her in. Pop never recovered from losing Gram. He started to go downhill right after that," Luke said.

"I am so sorry," is all that Addison could say. She was overwhelmed by what Luke had shared with her.

After a few moments of silence, Luke added, "I have a half-brother."

"Have you met him?" asked Addison.

"No," Luke replied, "but I am sure he will show up at my door someday."

Neither Luke nor Addison spoke for a few moments after that. It was awkward and Addison felt a little uncomfortable. Luke obviously trusted her enough to share his darkest secret. She wanted him to know that she would never betray him.

"Okay," she finally said. "Rotten, selfish mother and worthless half-brother tops my cheating fiancé. You win. Next time bring wine, this is too heavy for just beer."

Luke grinned. The tightness in his neck and face seemed to relax again.

"Speaking of beer..." he said as he reached down into the cooler.

"I don't know why I told you all that," Luke said softly, "I have never told anyone," he said to Addison in earnest. "You're easy to talk to," he said as he gave her a small smile and touched her hands.

Without thinking, she put her arms around him and hugged him closely.

"Thank you," she whispered in his ear.

He had not felt such genuine comfort and caring from any woman since the passing of his grandmother. When they finally broke away from the embrace, he thought to himself, maybe it's the apron with the little white flowers.

# CHAPTER NINETEEN

Luke and Miles had just come into the house. They had been riding around the ranch checking on some calves that had recently been born. It was a hot afternoon. They each had a tall cold glass of sweet tea, and they were enjoying the air conditioning in the living room where they were sitting with Henry and Addison.

Henry was sitting in his favorite chair, sleeping, and Addison was watching a game between the Yankees and the Reds on television. It was the bottom of the seventh and the score was tied.

"If you liked football, as much as you like baseball, I might marry you," Luke said with a laugh as he picked up the newspaper.

Miles shouted out, "drop it, drop it," as the Yankee outfielder dashed to catch a fly ball the Red's batter had hit. He knew it would irritate Addison. She gave him a half smirk as the television showed a replay of the ball dropping into the outfielder's glove.

Maria entered the room carrying a large bouquet of flowers surrounding a little Happy Birthday balloon.

"It's for Miss Addison," Maria announced as she carried

them over to the side table next to the chair where Addison was sitting. She smiled at Addison and told her how pretty the flowers looked and wished her a happy birthday before leaving the room.

"Is it your birthday?" Luke asked, sounding surprised. "Why didn't you say anything?"

Addison was a bit embarrassed. She shrugged and told them all that it wasn't a big deal.

"It is too a big deal, and I feel really badly that we didn't know," Luke told her. He then turned to Miles, and said, "You're falling down on the job buddy, you're supposed to keep up with these things."

Miles didn't say anything, but Addison could tell that he too genuinely felt badly.

"Who are they from?" Luke asked.

Addison opened the small card that was attached to the bouquet.

"My folks," Addison replied with a smile on her face.

The commotion woke up Henry, who complimented her on the pretty flowers. He left the room for a few moments and when he came back, he handed Addison a card and a box of Russell Stover milk chocolates that he had asked Travis to pick up for him.

"It would be okay with me if you want to open them now," Henry told her.

Addison laughed, opened the box, and offered Henry a piece of candy. She read his card, and gave him a gentle hug, thanking him.

"I feel terrible," Luke said. "Let me make it up to you," he started to say just as Maria entered the room again with another bouquet of flowers.

Luke crossed his arms and shot Miles a look of pure dissatisfaction.

"Who are those from" Miles asked. "Probably that preacher that keeps hanging around," he said, answering his own question.

"Pop, how did you know it was Addison's birthday?" Luke asked his grandfather while Addison opened the card that came with the flowers.

"Pastor Rich had a cake for her at seniors," Pop answered as he picked out another piece of candy.

"A party, even better than flowers," Miles said just to irritate his friend.

Luke shot him an exasperated look, and said to his grandfather, "Why didn't you say something?"

"Thought you knew," was Henry's reply.

These flowers were from Maggie Grace, and the card said, "I won't take no for an answer."

"No for what answer?" Luke inquired.

Addison explained that Maggie Grace had insisted on taking Addison out for her birthday. Addison quickly added that she had not planned on going and that she and Pop were going to watch a movie and make popcorn.

"You call her right now, and tell her that you are going out," Luke said firmly. "I mean it! Let me know where you are going, so I can get Travis to drive you," he added.

Travis dropped Addison off at *Doppel's a* new karaoke bar that had recently opened. Maggie Grace, her husband, Nate, and his sister, Lori were there waiting. Nate was a successful real estate broker that specialized in commercial buildings. One of his clients had recently purchased the bar and had been anxious for Nate to see it. Lori had been one of Maggie's bridesmaids when she married Nate, and Addison had known her for a long time. She was glad to see her. Lori had recently divorced, and obviously started the birthday celebration two drinks sooner than Addison's arrival.

Miles had called Maggie Grace to find out where they would be, and to tell her that he and Luke planned on crashing the party, if she didn't mind. She was thrilled with the idea and promised not to say anything to Addison.

The bar had a $20 cover charge. A large, gruff looking man at the door handed Luke a card with the number thirty-four written on.

"What's this?" Luke asked.

"That's when you go on," the man replied with a tone that implied that Luke was an idiot.

Luke and Miles looked at each other in puzzlement and then back at the man.

"You singin' tonight, or what?" the man said with an annoyed tone. "You got your music with you?" he asked.

"I wasn't planning on singing," Luke said dumbfounded.

The man looked him up and down.

"Too bad. You almost look like the real thing," he said as he snatched the numbered card out of Luke's hands and moved so that Luke and Miles could enter the bar.

The ambience was much like any other bar. The lights were dim, and the air smelled like stale beer. Thankfully, smoking was prohibited. Miles and Luke stopped dead in their tracks when they saw what appeared to be Dolly Parton on stage singing "Jolene." They looked at each other in disbelief until Miles caught sight of two more Dolly Partons sitting in the audience. Looking around, they noticed three Kenny Chesneys, a Keith Urban, three Carrie Underwoods, four Chers, two Elvises, and three looked like Johnny Cash. More than half the people in the bar were dressed up like celebrities.

They spied Addison and her friends and quickly made it over to her table. She was genuinely excited to see them. Luke pulled his chair up next to Addison's and Nate moved closer to Maggie Grace so that Miles could slide in next to Lori.

"Isn't this place amazing," Addison said to Luke as she explained the connection between Nate and the owner.

Luke had to agree. With so many celebrity look-a-likes, no one paid any attention to him. It was great. There were no photographers trying to catch him in awkward poses and none of the customers seemed to recognize him.

Prior to each act, the announcer called out a number. It was time for number twenty-three to perform. A young curly haired blond girl got up and started singing *Chains,* doing her best to sound and look like Carole King.

*"Chains, my baby's got me locked up in chains,*
*And they ain't the kind that you can see."*

As the singer continued belting out the song, Luke took hold of Addison's hand and brought her up to the dance floor. They danced through that song and the next three. Little Eva's *Loco-motion*, Shawn Menders' *Senorita* and *7 Rings* by Arianna Grande.

To their surprise, the next singer was Luke Johnson. Addison and Luke looked at each other and started to laugh.

"I hope he doesn't sound better than me," Luke said.

"I hope he does *Gather My Soul*, that is such a beautiful love song, makes me cry." she whispered into Luke's ear.

As if the wanna be musician read her mind, the melody of the song began, and he started singing the lyrics. Luke gently pulled Addison into his arm as she laid her head on his shoulder for the slow dance. He felt her warm breath on his neck, and he could smell the aroma of jasmine in her hair. When she lifted her head and looked up into his eyes, he had to resist the strong urge to kiss her. She smiled sweetly at him and then rested her head on his chest as their bodies shifted to get closer. They lingered entwined with each other on the dance floor through the last chord of the song.

After that song, the couple returned to the table to join their friends. Miles and Lori had also been dancing. She was getting pretty wasted, and during the last slow dance, Luke noticed that the two of them were wrapped pretty tightly during the number. Sitting at the table now, Miles had his arm around the back of Lori's waist. Nate and Magnolia had just returned to the table after taking some time to speak with the owner, Nate's client, who was standing at the bar. Nate had wanted to introduce Magnolia to him.

Luke ordered another round of drinks for the table and some more food items to snack on. Addison noticed that Luke ordered a Coke for himself, and Miles had barely touched his last beer. Both men knew the potential consequences to Luke's career if he ever got a DUI or was seen drunk in public. They were careful to limit their consumption to no more than one beer an hour while out in public, and to stop drinking at least an hour before driving. The waitress came back with baskets of wings, French fried potatoes dripping with cheese sauce, nachos, and a bucket of steamed shrimp.

"I am really sorry about today," Luke said quietly to Addison as he pulled a small blue Tiffany's box out of the inside pocket of the jacket he had draped over the back of his chair.

"You did not have to get me anything," Addison told him. "Just all of us going out, made the day pretty perfect," she added as she unwrapped the gift.

Inside the box was a pair of diamond stud earrings.

"This is too much," she said protesting the beautiful gift.

"Just wait for Christmas," Miles chirped in as he reached across the table to also give Addison a small gift.

Inside the box, was a wallet size photo of Miles.

"I wanted to give you something that I knew you didn't already have," Miles said.

Everyone at the table burst out laughing. After which, Miles and Lori disappeared outside for a few minutes to get some fresh air, and Luke left the table to head for the door marked, "Cowboys".

Magnolia leaned towards Addison and said,

"What do you think Judy, do the best things happen while your dancing?"

Both of the women laughed.

"Why yes, Betty. I think they do." Addison replied as the women shared another burst of laughter.

This was a secret code the two of them had used in college to size up the dates they had. It was based on one of the songs from "White Christmas" a movie they loved, and still watched every December.

If one of them started singing or humming "Snow" it

meant let's get out of here fast. "Love You Didn't Do Right By Me" meant the guy was a dud and the "Best Things" indicated that the guy and the evening were great.

Luke returned to the table where the girls were still laughing, Addison stretched her arms around her best friend who started kissing her on the cheeks and forehead.

"Okay, that's enough you two," Nate said pulling his wife back towards him. Still laughing, the young women began singing in unison,

*"Lord help the Mister,*
*that comes between me and my sister,*
*and Lord help the sister,*
*that comes between me and my man."*

Nate shook his head at Luke, who was obviously totally at a loss as to what the girls were doing or talking about. All he knew was that Addison seemed to be having a wonderful time, and he was glad to be part of it.

The evening ended with the waitress bringing out a birthday cake, which they enjoyed, after everyone at the table sang the traditional "Happy Birthday" song. A large number of other patrons sitting near their table also joined in the singing.

The owner came over with a bottle of champaign. He told them that the man that looked like Kenny Chesney, who was sitting at the bar, had sent it over with a note for Miles.

"Good to see you, old buddy, tell that imposter sitting with you that he's with the prettiest girl here. See you all at the CMA's."

After Miles and Luke read the note, they turned, nodded

and smiled at their real friend who had sent it over. Luke gave a motion to invite Kenny over, but he declined with a smile. It seems they both thought this was a great bar for a night out incognito.

The small party talked for a few minutes outside the bar before going to their cars. Nate and Maggie Grace were trying to coax Lori into riding home with them, but she refused. Miles handed Luke the keys to his CJ7 and told him that he felt Lori shouldn't drive, so he was going to drive her car and take her home.

"I'll catch an UBER later," Miles said to Luke.

"You're a real Boy Scout," Luke said back to his friend as Miles was walking towards Lori.

Luke held the door open and helped Addison into the front seat of the Jeep. She, too, was a bit tipsy from the evening festivities.

Addison stretched out in the bucket seat. Kicking off her sandals, she placed one foot on the dash. She was unusually chatty during the ride home, and frequently started to sing some of the songs they had heard in the bar.

*"My little baby sister can do with ease*
*Come on baby do the locomotion.*
*It's easier than learning your ABC's now,*
*Come on baby do the locomotion."*

Addison was singing the words and swaying in her seat. Luke smiled.

"Hey sing with me," she said to Luke.

"What do you have in mind?"

Addison thought for a moment and then began singing

Kenny Rogers' song from *The Gambler,* with Luke joining in,

*"You got to know when to hold up*
*Know when to fold up*
*Know when to walk away*
*Know when to run*
*You never count your money*
*While you're sitting at the table*
*There will be time enough for counting*
*When the dealings done"*

When they finished, she started laughing about her singing a duet with Luke Johnson.

"I think we make beautiful music together," he replied.

"Do you think it's hot in here?" Addison asked playing with the electric window opener. A gust of wind blew into the car, blowing her long hair back, and her skirt up to her thigh.

Luke used the control on the driver's door to partially close the window, and then reached over to pull Addison's skirt back down, even though he had enjoyed looking at the exposed skin.

"Why did the Yankees have to lose on my birthday?" she asked Luke, pouting a bit.

"I don't know," he replied. "It certainly was very rude of them," he said, trying to sound serious.

"It was rude," Addison exclaimed. After a few moments, she said, "But you know what" she asked giggling.

"What," Luke answered.

"I still had the best birthday, ever," she stated.

"I'm glad," he replied back.

"I'm glad you came. You and Miles. I'm glad you both came. Did you plan on coming? Why didn't you tell me you were coming?" Addison was rattling off the comments and questions as she leaned towards the driver.

Luke was enjoying this. He had never seen Addison like this before. He was glad he did go, and he was glad that he was driving her home.

"We worked it out with Magnolia," he said to her.

"Oh, Maggie Grace, she is my best friend, I just love her, don't you love Maggie Grace too?" she said to Luke.

"Yes, I just love her," Luke repeated, smiling.

Addison pulled the two small boxes out of her purse and opened the one from Miles. She laughed again when she saw the picture.

"He doesn't give those to just anybody, I guess you've made the grade," Luke said with a smile.

Addison reflected on Luke and Miles' relationship. He wasn't really an employee, although he did earn a paycheck from Luke. He was not Luke's manager, stagehand, or ranch foreman. As if reading her mind, Luke shared his thoughts about Miles.

"He is the best friend I could possibly have," Luke told her. "He is loyal, he handles a lot of stuff for me. I guess you could say he keeps me honest and grounded," Luke stated.

"How so?" Addison asked him.

"In this business, a lot of people want to be your friend, but it's all about the money and the fame. Miles was my friend before any of this Luke Johnson stuff happened. He's not afraid to tell me like it is, and to knock me on my butt if I need it. When he tells me something, even if he tells me I am screwing something up, I know it's the truth. I know he is telling me, whatever it is, out of friendship. He's a good judge of people too. So that picture he gave you, that really means, he's got your back too," Luke said sincerely.

"Well, he didn't do a good job with that Barbie Jo," Addison said. "She was horrible," she added shaking her head.

Luke nodded. He was surprised that Addison mentioned Barbie Jo and wasn't sure where that came from.

"That is all on me," Luke said. "Miles told me she was bad news, and I didn't listen."

"Well, you should have. You should always listen to Miles," Addison said as she turned to look out of the window.

"What does Miles say about me?" she asked.

"He says, you should not have more than three Margaritas," Luke said, laughing, to which, Addison started singing Shelly West's song "Jose Cuervo".

*"Jose Cuervo you are a friend of mine*
*I like to drink you with a little salt and lime*
*Did I kiss all the cowboys?*
*Did I shoot out the lights?*
*Did I dance on the bar?*
*Did I start any fights?"*

Luke laughed. "You better not kiss all the cowboys," he told her.

"There is only one cowboy I want to kiss," she replied and then started giggling again, as if she alone was privy to a great secret.

Addison reached into her purse and pulled out her wallet. She slid the picture of Miles into one of the plastic photo sleeves and dropped the wallet back into her purse. Next, she opened the small blue Tiffany box that Luke had given her. She ran her fingers over the glistening stones and smiled at him. Pulling the visor down and sliding open the lighted mirror she carefully replaced the earrings she had worn with the ones Luke had given her.

"They are beautiful," she said to him, "thank you so much."

"You are beautiful," he replied.

Addison was feeling a little lightheaded, so when Luke stretched out his hand to hold hers, she smiled, enjoying his firm grip. When they parked the jeep, Luke came around to help her out. He put his arms around her waist and carefully lifted her down to the pavement. They lingered in the embrace.

Addison looked at him, and then tossed her arms around his neck and kissed him.

"You are the only cowboy I want to kiss," she said and kissed him again.

Luke was taken by surprise, but he was certainly enjoying Addison's lack of inhibition brought about by the libations she had consumed.

She pressed her body closely into his, kissing him again.

"Jimmy Lukens," she said as she gazed into his eyes, "I really love you," she said softly.

He wanted her, and surprised himself when he unlocked the arms she had around his neck, and stepped back away from her.

"I think we better get you to bed," he said.

"I feel a little dizzy," she replied, and then lost her balance as she tried to take a step towards the porch.

Luke swept her up into his arms and carried her into the house and to her bedroom. Her head rested on his shoulder, and he could feel her soft breathing on his neck. With one hand he pulled the covers down on the bed while juggling her limp body with the other. He laid her down, hesitating as he thought whether to remove her dress or not. He decided not to and pulled the covers up to her chin. She was already in peaceful sleep.

"Happy birthday," Luke said softly and then gently kissed her forehead.

Henry had gone to bed some hours earlier. Dale and Raymond had come up to the house and played cards with him until about nine. They offered to stay if Henry wanted them to, but he was in good spirits. He knew Luke and Miles had headed out to surprise Addison and he did not want to be a bother to anyone.

"I don't need a damn babysitter," he told Raymond. "They put up the matches and the sharp knives, so I guess I will be okay," he added. By the time Addison and Luke got home, Henry was sleeping peacefully.

Luke lay in his bed. He could not stop thinking about Addison. He could still taste her lips on his. He still could feel how tightly she had pressed her body into his, and how much he wanted her. He was glad he had stopped. He knew it was the right thing to do but wondered what it would be like if he had given into his desires. She told him she loved him. Would she remember that in the morning he wondered? A lot of women had told Luke Johnson that they loved him, but Addison, had told Jimmy Lukens. That was different. That was him, not some persona made up to promote an image. Why did this feel so different? He tossed and turned, re-asking himself the same questions over and over.

# CHAPTER TWENTY

Luke was set to perform at the Nissan Stadium in Nashville Labor Day weekend. The concert had been sold out for months. After that, Luke planned to take a week off before going into the recording studio, doing some fall TV appearances and the last leg of his concerts for the year. During his break, he, Addison, Miles and Pop would drive to Roanoke, VA.

They would go with Pop to put flowers on Alice's grave. Luke would do a small concert for the vets at the VA Hospital in Salem, and on September 11th he would help with the Relay for Life event held annually at Lord Botetourt, his high school alma mater.

Pop would stay at the family farm in Botetourt County, where Luke had grown up, until early November when Luke's touring season ended. Addison would have her paid vacation time while Henry was at the farm with his sister Helen.

When Luke reminded her of the upcoming break, Addison did not feel she needed a vacation and felt sadness when she thought of being away from everyone. Her parents were in Australia so she was not sure where she would spend her time off. They had encouraged her to join them, but she just didn't want to be a half a world away from Luke, Henry and even Miles.

She thought about spending the time with Maggie Grace and her family.

Luke left to go to the concert venue around 3:00 that afternoon. Pop wore himself out telling Addison stories about growing up in Virginia as they looked through a photo album that Alice had assembled. Henry got frustrated from time to time as he stared at a picture but could not recall who was in it. Thankfully, Alice had put the dates and names on the back of the photos.

There were a lot of photos of John Lukens as he grew up. It was the first time that Addison had seen what Luke's father really looked like. She recognized the blue eyes and wide smile that Luke had inherited. Both men seemed to be about the same size and build. When she asked about seeing photos of Luke, Pop replied that Jimmy was in another album, and he would try to find it. He said it might still be at the farm.

By 8:00 in the evening, the concert was underway, and Pop had headed to bed. Looking at the photos made her nostalgic for her family. Addison decided to sit at the beautiful desk in her bedroom and write an e-mail to her parents. She wanted to know how their trip was going. She was startled when her personal cell phone rang. Her parents and Maggie Grace were the only people that called her on it. She withdrew the phone from the nightstand next to her bed. She glanced at the number and saw that it was Maggie Grace.

"Hey Girl," she said cheerfully, only to be immediately interrupted by her frantic sounding friend.

"Oh my God! Is he okay? Have you heard anything?" Maggie Grace was almost hysterical.

"Is who okay? Heard what?" was Addison's reply.

"Oh, Sweet Jesus," said her friend. "You don't know? Quick turn on the TV. Luke Johnson was just shot on stage."

"Luke...Shot...No," her voice trailed off as she sat down numbly on her bed.

At that moment, the cell phone that Miles had given her months before started ringing.

"Hold on," she told her friend. She did not recognize the number, but she answered it immediately.

"Addison Albright?" asked the voice on the other end.

"Yes," she replied.

"This is Sharon from Vanderbilt University Medical Center."

"Oh God, Luke, is Luke there? Is he okay," she gasped into the phone?

"Mr. Johnson listed you as his emergency contact. He is going into surgery, and he insisted that we call and tell you," the voice said.

"Surgery? Is he okay, how badly hurt is he? Is Miles with him?" she asked.

"I can't discuss his condition on the phone. If you come to the hospital, you will need to have photo ID, or we will not be able to let you see him. There is a lot of press here." Sharon said, with an excited tone. "It is very hectic."

"Ok, thanks, I will be there as soon as possible," Addison said, hanging up the phone.

"Maggie Grace," she said into the other line, " I gotta go, I will call you back as soon as I can."

Addison thought for a moment trying to calmly collect herself and decide what to do next. She called Raymond's number.

"Yes ma'am," he said when he picked up the phone. "I saw it on the TV and was just about to come up to check on you. What do you need?" Raymond's steady voice asked.

"I need you to come up to the house. Pop is in bed, and I don't want to tell him anything right now. I don't know what to tell him. I have to get to the hospital. I think Pop will stay in bed, but in case he gets up, I need someone here."

"Yes ma'am, I will be right up," Raymond said and then hung up his line.

The next number she called was Travis. He too had heard the news and was already on route to the ranch.

"I need a ride to the hospital, right away," she said. "Something the press won't recognize, like the Silverado."

No one would expect her to show up in a pickup truck, she thought to herself.

With both men on their way to the house, she rushed into Luke's room. She pulled some clean socks, underwear and tee shirts from his dresser and grabbed two shirts and a pair of jeans from his closet. She went into his bathroom and reached for his toothbrush, paste, hairbrush, comb and deodorant. She threw the items in the gym bag in his closet and added a couple of pairs of the boxers he liked to sleep in.

He will want his own things she said to herself, trying to calm down as she zipped the bag closed. Maybe sneakers, she thought, he only had his boots with him.

She tiptoed past Pop's room stopping at her own. She grabbed a tote bag from her closet and threw in both cell phones and the sneakers that would not fit in the bag she packed for Luke. She picked up her purse, making sure her wallet was in it, her ID, some cash and a charge card in case she needed anything.

She had the house keys and her hairbrush in the purse as well. She reached into her closet and pulled out a light sweater.

A few seconds later she was waiting at the front door. Travis pulled up as Raymond was getting out of his jeep.

"I'll take that bag, ma'am," Raymond said as he took the gym bag from Addison's hand. "He's just gonna be fine," Raymond was saying to her as she climbed up into the Chevy. "Don't worry about Pop, I'll take good care of him."

Addison stopped for a second. "What will you tell him if he wakes up and Luke and I aren't here?" she asked.

"I'll tell him the two of you run off and eloped. That would make him very happy," Raymond said as he shut the Chevy door.

Addison's mouth dropped and she was at a loss for a reply. Travis hit the gas and they were speeding down the long driveway in seconds. He hit a remote that he held in his hand and the front gates opened. A swarm of photographers and news media were already camped at the end of the driveway. When Travis saw them, he told Addison to put her head down.

"Unless you want your picture on the front-page tomorrow," he said to her.

Addison leaned over and lowered her head so that it appeared to be just Travis in the vehicle. She looked at her watch. It had been 14 minutes since the call from Maggie Grace came in. Everything was happening so fast. For the first time she was able to take a breath and the news fully sank in. Tears swelled up in her eyes and she quietly started to sob.

"He's going to be just fine," Travis tried to reassure her.

"I know," she managed to say. "It's just that I don't know how bad it is. They wouldn't tell me on the phone. Did I tell you

Vanderbilt?" she asked Travis.

"No, but I figured as much. It will take us about 30 minutes to get there. Don't get rattled by the reporters," he added.

"Has this happened before? You sound like you..." she began, unable to finish the sentence.

"No," he quickly said. "But we all have emergency training."

"I will let you out here," Travis told her as he pulled up to the emergency room door. Text me when you find out where he is and let me know, okay? Don't look at the reporters or let them know who you are here for."

Addison nodded as she climbed out of the truck. She walked up to the triage station nurse and leaned in to speak to her.

'I'm Addison Albright," she said quietly. "Sharon called me to come to the hospital. I am listed as the emergency contact for," she stopped and leaned in even further, whispering the name Luke Johnson.

The admitting clerk looked at her with a judgmental eye. "Photo ID please."

Addison pulled her wallet out of her purse and handed her driver's license to the young clerk at the desk.

"This says you live in New York," the woman said curtly. "What is your relationship with the patient? Visitation is only for immediate family."

"He asked for me. He listed me as his emergency contact." Addison was feeling a little annoyed.

"What is your relationship?" the triage clerk asked again with a solemn face.

Addison knew if she said she was his grandfather's

assistant that she would never get through the door.

"We live together," she said firmly.

The clerk raised her eyebrow and looked at her.

Addison was fully agitated.

"Who is in charge here? What is your full name?" Addison asked. "Mr. Johnson makes sizable donations to this hospital and if he stops, I want him to be able to say why."

Addison did not recognize the voice or tone that was coming from her lips. The clerk, however, quickly changed her demeanor.

"Please come in through the doors on my left," the woman said.

"Hey, did that lady say she lives with Luke Johnson?" a reporter said to the photographer standing with him. "Quick get a picture."

When the first flash went off the crowd of reporters turned their attention to Addison and tried to swarm around her. She reached the door and was buzzed in by the nurse just in time to escape the torrid of questions. A hospital representative greeted her on the other side of the door and the triage clerk went back to her station. When she did, the reporters clamored to get more information from her.

The young woman was obviously enjoying the attention. She revealed that the woman's name was Addison Albright, that her license said she lived in New York and that she claimed to be living with Luke Johnson. The next day the clerk would be referred to as "a reliable source close to Ms. Albright," in the morning papers.

Within seconds Smartphones were engaged to find more information about this pretty mystery woman. Someone found a picture of her with a New York Yankee outfielder. Someone else found that they were once engaged. Another added that sources said the engagement was broken off due to possible infidelity in the relationship.

Within minutes, the group had concluded that America's Prince of Country had broken up the engagement because of an illicit affair with the woman he was now living with, probably the same woman that broke up his engagement to Barbie Jo Bentley.

Addison followed the young man that had met her at the door. He stopped at the entrance of a small private waiting room.

"Where is Luke? What is happening? How is he? No one is telling me anything," she said with frustration.

The man indicated that Addison should sit down. He then began to give her a progress report. Mr. Johnson was shot by someone in the crowd at the concert. He had surgery to remove a bullet from his right leg. It does not appear that the bullet hit any vital organs or that the wound is life-threatening."

Addison gave a deep sigh of relief. "Why didn't they tell me that on the phone, instead of causing all this anxiety," she said.

"HIPAA laws, we have to be careful," was the reply.

The young man continued, "Mr. Johnson had surgery to remove the bullet. He did lose quite a bit of blood, and the shot knocked him off his feet. When he fell on the stage, he hit his head pretty badly. The doctor was concerned about brain hemorrhaging so he also ordered a CAT scan. We will have to monitor him for a day or so."

"What about Miles Wilcox?" Addison asked. The young

man gritted his teeth before answering.

"His condition is a little more serious," he said with a grim face. Mr. Wilcox took a bullet in the shoulder. He's lucky it did not hit his neck, that could have been fatal. He's going to need a more complicated surgery, but we have to stabilize him first. After that, he will need a great deal of rehab."

Tears filled Addison's eyes and she tried to blink them away.

"Mr. Wilcox saved Mr. Johnson's life," the young man continued. The projection of the second bullet would have hit Mr. Johnson in the head."

"Oh Miles," Addison whispered. "Where is he, can I see him too?"

"Not yet, his surgery will probably take about six hours, and then he will be in ICU for a few days."

"Can we go, can I see Luke yet?" she asked.

"In just a minute. There is a police officer here that wants to ask you a few questions."

"Me? Why?" she asked with astonishment.

"I will be right back, he is just outside," the young man said as he opened the door and left Addison alone for a few moments.

Detective Tran came into the room. He was a tall man with slightly graying hair.

"I am sorry to keep you, Ms. Albright, I know you are anxious to see your loved ones," the detective said to Addison.

The two talked for about ten minutes. When he left the room, the young administrator returned.

"Mr. Johnson is in recovery now," he told her. "I will take you up to him. He has had his CAT scan so they will probably give him some more pain medicine and something to help him sleep. You won't be able to stay long."

Addison stood at the door of Luke's recovery room. Luke still had an IV taped to the back side of his hand. In the corner of the room was a plastic basin with Luke's blood-soaked clothes heaped into it. The sight made Addison feel weak.

"You're here," Luke said reaching his hand out to her.

She walked over to him and took his hand in hers.

"Oh Luke," she said, her eyes filling with tears. "I was so worried," she managed to say before bursting into sobs.

He pulled her closer so she could sit on the edge of the bed.

"It's okay, Sugar," he said softly.

She buried her head in Luke's chest as he stroked her hair. "It's okay," he said again.

"I don't know what I would do if something happened to you," she said between sobs, crying so hard that she had to catch her breath.

She lifted her head as his hand moved down to caress her face. He brushed away her tears and pulled her close to him. He looked deeply into her eyes, and gently kissed her. She wrapped her arms around his neck and held him closely.

"It's okay," he repeated. "I am gonna be fine."

She nodded with her head still nuzzled against his neck.

"Who's with Pop?" he asked her.

"Raymond," she replied. "Travis is waiting downstairs."

Luke nodded.

"Have you heard anything about Miles?" he asked.

"Yes," and she reported what the hospital administrator had told her.

"Anything he needs. Anything," Luke repeated firmly.

"You tell them, okay, anything. I have it covered. Make sure they know that, okay." His voice was anxious.

"A police detective was asking me questions about the shooting," she told him.

"You, why?" he said puzzled.

"They wanted to know if I thought you had a relationship with the suspect's wife," Addison said.

"What?" Luke answered with a look of sheer astonishment on his face.

"It seems," she continued, "the wife is really obsessed with you. She went to nine of your concerts this year. She ran up $40,000 buying tickets to the concerts, travel expenses and hotels. Maxed out their charge cards and a chunk of their home equity line."

"She must be nuts," Luke responded.

"Last week, when she was, you know, being intimate with her husband, she yelled out your name, and that pushed her husband over the edge."

"They are both nuts!" Luke said shaking his head.

"Well thanks to the hundred or so fans illegally filming your concert on their phones, the police have footage of the entire shootings, and so does Facebook and Instagram."

"I hope they hang the bastard," Luke was saying when a doctor in green scrubs entered the room.

The doctor nodded at Addison and then introduced himself, "Mr. Johnson, I am Dr. Youmans," he said walking up to the patient. "I did your surgery."

Luke reached out to shake the doctor's hand.

"How are you feeling?" he asked his patient.

"Like Hell," was Luke's reply, "and really, really lucky," he quickly added.

The doctor nodded. "You were really lucky. The bullet missed all major arteries, and the CAT scan is clear. I am going to give you some Oxycontin for the pain, and to help you sleep. They will put it in your IV. Do you have any questions for me?"

"Miles, what is happening with him?" Luke asked.

"He's comfortable. Due to the nature of the wound, we need to wait until morning to operate. Dr. Welsh will head up that surgery. She is the top orthopedic doctor in Nashville. His injuries are more serious, and I think he will be here for a while before we release him to rehab. He is sedated and sleeping. The bullet first hit his shoulder and then passed through and shattered his wrist.

"Anything he needs...." Luke told the doctor.

"We are going to let you get some sleep now, and I think in a couple of days you can go home providing you have someone there to take care of you."

"I've got the best," he said looking over at Addison.

The doctor smiled at her. "I will let you both say goodnight, and then we better let you get some sleep. You too miss, it's been a long night and you need to get some rest too. Come back in the morning after you have had some time to sleep."

The doctor left them alone to say goodbye as the nurse came in to add the medicine to the IV.

"When you come tomorrow, will you bring me some things from home?"

"I have some, Travis has them in the truck." She pulled out her phone and sent him a text message with the room number. The medicine had already kicked in and Luke was sleeping by the time Travis made it to the room.

"He's okay," Addison told Travis who was obviously relieved by the news.

"Miles?" Travis asked.

"I'll tell you on the ride home," Addison said. She glanced at her watch. It was a little after 3 in the morning.

# CHAPTER TWENTY-ONE

Addison left Raymond sleeping on the couch and quietly went to her room. She was exhausted, but sleep did not immediately come. She replayed all the events of the night, but the ones she kept coming back to her were the kiss that Luke had given her, and what lay ahead for Miles. Her short three hours of sleep ended when she heard Pop talking to Raymond.

"Let's make some coffee," she heard Raymond say to Pop.

"But where's Addison and Jimmy?" he asked Raymond again.

Addison put her robe on and tried to shake the sleep from her eyes. She came into the kitchen and found the two men sipping on cups of steaming coffee.

"Everything okay?" Raymond asked as Addison walked over to the Keurig.

"Yes. Thank you. Travis can fill you in, okay? I think I need to talk to Pop."

Raymond took one more big gulp of coffee and stood up to go. "See you at the barn, Pop," he said, "and if you need anything, just let me know," he told Addison as he left the room.

"Thanks for everything," Addison called after him.

Pop was sitting at the table. He had pushed his chair back and his arms were folded across his chest. He looked carefully at Addison. He had never seen her look so tired and worn out, he thought to himself. She had not taken the time to comb her hair or get dressed before breakfast. Her eyes were puffy. The dark circles beneath them emphasized her exhaustion and it was evident that she had been crying. He knew something terrible must have happened. He wanted to know, but he was afraid of what it might be.

"Pop," Addison said, pulling her chair up close to his. "Something bad happened last night."

Henry stared at her. "To Jimmy?" he asked with a hushed tone.

"Yes. But he's okay," she quickly added."

Henry exhaled the breath he had been holding and looked relieved.

"And to Miles. But he's not as okay as Jimmy," she said slowly.

"Just tell me," Pop said with a calm voice that Addison had not heard before. "I can take it."

Addison told him about the crazed husband and the shooting. She described Luke's injuries and the heroism that Miles displayed saving Luke's life. She started to cry again. She could not shake the thought of what might have happened that kept running through her mind.

Henry reached over to her and wrapped his arms around her. Her face was buried in his shoulder as she wept. She knew that it should have been her comforting him, but she was too emotionally weak to do that. He let her cry and patted her back until the sobs became tears that finally subsided. She finally lifted her head and looked searchingly into his face.

"We're going to eat a little breakfast, and then you get showered and dressed," he told her with new authority in his voice. "Can Travis drive us, or do you think he is too tired? We can get one of the other fellows you know," Henry said.

"Travis told me to call him when I was ready to go back," she told him.

"We will call him when you get out of the shower," he told her as he walked to the counter and brought over a plate of blueberry muffins and two bananas.

"He might as well sleep as long as he can," Henry told her. "It's gonna be a long day, and you need to keep your strength up," he said to Addison.

"Do you want eggs or anything?" he asked her.

She said no and began to peel one of the bananas. Addison was not used to Pop being strong and taking charge. She did not know where it was coming from, but she was thankful for it.

The drive to the hospital seemed to take an eternity. Henry could see that Travis looked worn out too. He had not shaved or showered and by the looks of it was wearing clothes that he had slept in. Henry told him that after he dropped them off at the hospital, to go back to the ranch and get some sleep. He instructed Travis to come back around three. That would give Travis a chance to sleep about five hours. He told him to come up to Luke's room when he came back to pick them up.

"I'm sure Luke will be glad to see you, and maybe by then, we will have some more news on him and Miles," Henry told Travis.

When they arrived at the hospital, Henry immediately

walked to the nurse's station.

"I want to see my grandson," he stated. What room is he in?"

That worried Addison. Henry's actions had been so unpredictable the entire morning. He had just told Travis Luke's room number. How could he have forgotten it ten minutes later, she thought. They had talked in the car about keeping low key and avoiding the reporters that were still lingering in the reception area trying to get information for their newspapers and tabloids.

"His name?" the receptionist asked.

Addison wanted to warn Pop to not say Luke's name loudly. Instead, she heard him say Miles Wilcox.

"He's in ICU, but only family are admitted to see him, and he has none listed on his record."

"Damn it, I am his grandfather, didn't you hear me?" Pop said with an agitated tone.

"Yes sir," the young girl said meekly. "3rd Floor, West elevator, ICU room 5."

Pop turned to Addison and told her to go check on Jimmy while he checked on Miles.

"I will meet you in Jimmy's room," he whispered to her as they walked towards the elevator.

She was still bewildered and at the same time thankful for his clarity and assertiveness. She felt comforted by it.

Luke smiled when he saw Addison. She was relieved to see him awake, and with some color back in his face. Both a nurse and a CNA were attending to him.

"Just had the best sponge bath of my life," Luke said obviously for the benefit of the two young women that were caring for him. They both blushed, giggled and told him if he needed anything to just ring the call button. They left his room, still giggling with each other.

Luke laughed when Addison told him about Pop.

"He's always been great in an emergency; it is the day to day living he can't handle," Luke told her.

"You look tired," he said. "There is no need to worry, I am fine," he added giving her a reassuring smile.

About an hour later, Henry entered Luke's room. He, too, looked worn out, but his spirits lifted when he saw how well Luke appeared.

"He's still in recovery," Henry said referring to Miles. You doing okay, boy?" he asked, reaching out to touch Luke's hand.

After assurances from Luke, Henry sat down in the large reclining chair next to Luke's bed. Luke pressed the call button, and three members of the nursing staff quickly came to his room to see what he needed. Luke requested some Ginger Ale for his grandfather and Addison and told the girls he would love a cold beer and a steak. They all thought that was hilarious and quickly left and returned with the soda.

Pop shared the information he had learned while waiting for Miles.

"It's not as bad as they first thought," he told Luke and Addison, sounding relieved. "The bullet went through his shoulder and did a number on his rotator cuff. They had to reattach the shoulder muscles and tendons. It looks like he had his arms stretched out, kinda like taking a dive towards you Luke, so when the bullet exited his shoulder, it hit his wrist and shattered the bone. He's gonna be in a lot of pain for a few days."

Henry added that Miles would have a cast on for a while and

probably be in a sling or something for a few months. After that, he would need another four to six months of physical therapy, Henry explained.

As bad as that was, there was a general sense of relief and a feeling of thankfulness that both Luke and Miles were much luckier than they could have been.

To everyone's surprise, a third visitor joined them. It was Pastor Rich. He had heard the news and wanted them all to know that he was there to help them with anything that they needed. He offered to bring Addison to the hospital if she needed someone to drive her. His well wishes were sincere, and they all prayed together. As he was leaving, to everyone's surprise, Henry told him that he might just see him Sunday morning in church.

# CHAPTER TWENTY-TWO

Luke used the remote and turned the hospital television on. He was amazed by the amount of coverage this event was creating. Reports with no or inaccurate information were being presented by reporters on the scene at the hospital, and others parked outside his Brentwood home.

Fans were driving up leaving flowers, candles, and photos of him outside the gates of his home. A clip of the security gate slowly opening to let Travis enter the driveway was shown. One fan was interviewed, a young guy in his twenties. A doe-eyed waif of a girl was hanging on his arm, crying.

"I just want to say to Luke, I hope you can hear us, we love you man," the fan said choking up.

"We are praying for you," the girl with him shouted into the microphone, her dark mascara running down her cheeks from crying.

The camera then panned the flowery shrine again. The next clip was back at the hospital. It showed Addison walking in the door.

"We believe this young woman is an intimate companion

to Mr. Johnson," the reporter said. "As soon as possible we hope to have an update from her. Currently she appears to be too distraught to talk about his condition."

"Christ, I'm not dead," Luke said flipping the channel only to find a similar "Breaking News' story about him there as well. He tossed the remote down.

"What are you going to tell them when you're not too distraught to talk about it?" Luke said with a laugh, looking at Addison.

"I am not going to tell them anything," she said.

"You have to now, they have you on camera. They will hound you to death if you don't," he told her.

"You really want me to say something to them?" she asked surprised.

"Yeah, it goes with the territory," he responded. "Sometimes it makes me crazy as hell, but if they didn't care, I would not have much of a career, would I," he told her.

"Now that they have a picture of, "my intimate friend", he repeated with a smile on his face, "they won't leave you alone."

Addison looked over at Henry. His head was laid back in the chair and he was snoring softly.

"If I have to do it, I'd rather not do it when Henry was with me. I don't think he needs that exposure, and they have not linked him to you yet," she said to Luke. "Don't you have some kind of PR person to do things like this?" she asked him.

"Of course, I do," he said, "but that is not the same as you doing it."

Addison, who had been sitting on the side of Luke's bed, stood up. She reached for her purse and pulled out the hairbrush and began brushing her hair.

"What are you doing?" Luke said looking puzzled.

"Well, if I have to do this, I am going to get it over with," she replied.

"Now?" he said surprised.

"Yes, now," she answered firmly. "Do I look okay?" she asked him.

"You look perfect," he told her.

Addison rode the elevator down to the hospital's lobby. She was nervous. Her heart was racing. She was silently trying to rehearse what she might say. The elevator doors opened, and she forced herself to step off onto the lobby floor. She just stood there, unable to move towards the waiting hacks and paparazzi. She did not have to wait long. Within moments they swarmed around her, asking questions with such rapid speed that she did not know where to start.

"What was her name?"

"That's not really important, aren't we hear to talk about Luke?" she answered back.

"What is your relationship to Luke Johnson?"

"I am just one of his employees," she responded.

"What is his condition?"

"He's stable and doing well. He also is greatly uplifted by the pouring in of good wishes, prayers and support that everyone is showing him," Addison said to them.

"He is especially appreciative of each you," she added, her palms facing upward as she fanned her hands towards the reporters.

"He appreciates how much you are doing to communicate his status to people that care about him."

This comment surprised the reporters, they were not used

to being "appreciated" for anything with celebrities.

"What about the other man that got shot, who is he?"

"He is another employee of Mr. Johnson, and I believe that he is doing well also."

"Who was that old man that came in with you?"

"Didn't he say he was the other man's grandfather?" She answered their question with a question. "I am really not authorized to answer any questions about Mr. Johnson's employees or their families," she stated.

"Is there anything special that Luke would want his fans to know?"

Addison thought for a moment.

"He is passionate about helping others. He loves the flowers that people have been leaving for him, but if anyone would like to show that they care and are thinking about him, then he asks that instead of flowers, canned goods be donated to a food bank near them," she told the reporters.

"In fact," she added, "there are already a lot of flowers and things that people are leaving out at the ranch. We are going to put up some large barrels instead so people can drop off canned goods in them if they want to show their love and support."

Flashes on the cameras and video recorders were about to blind her. The reporters were nodding their heads in approval for the food plea she was making, which started to make her feel even more confident in what she was saying.

"Luke weights about 220 pounds," Addison stated. Wouldn't it be great if we were able to collect 220 pounds of canned goods?" she said staring directly into the camera.

She then thanked everyone again for their concern as she pressed the elevator button to ride back up to Luke's room.

"How'd it go?" Luke asked her as soon as she entered the room.

Addison rolled her eyes.

"I was very nervous," she said.

"What did they ask you, what did you tell them?" Luke queried.

Addison looked at Luke. She was still feeling a little annoyed that he had sent her on that task.

"I told them you were near death. That you had a full body cast on, that you were suffering with amnesia, and that you thought you were Keith Urban," she said with a bit of sarcasm.

"I think Miles is rubbing off on you," he said with a laugh.

"Time for lunch," a middle-aged woman with a hair net on said when she entered the room carrying a tray. She set it on the table that swung across the hospital bed. The CNA was with her. The young girl adjusted Luke's bed so that he was more in an upright position to make it easier for him to eat and she fluffed the pillow behind him. She took the lids off the food items that had been delivered. Apple juice, milk, coffee, Salisbury steak with brown gravy, mashed potatoes, green beans and a piece of apple pie filled the tray.

The older woman and the CNA left but returned quickly carrying two more trays, each with the same items as Luke's.

"Here are the two extra lunches you ordered," the woman announced when they carried the food in.

Luke thanked them and noticed that the older woman put in her pocket the menu sheet that Luke had signed when he requested the extra meals.

Addison gently shook Henry's arm to wake him up. He smiled when he smelled the food.

"I've got to wash my hands," he said as he carefully got up from the recliner and went into the small private bathroom.

"They are supposed to take this damn catheter out this afternoon and get me out of bed and walking some," Luke said to Addison.

Before they had finished their lunch, beeping sounds could be heard coming from the TV with an announcer saying that they were interrupting the regularly scheduled broadcast with some breaking news. It was Addison's interview, and she was shocked at how quickly it was being played.

When it was done, Luke was speechless.

"Did I sound okay?" Addison asked. "God, I look awful," she said before Luke even had a chance to reply to the first question.

"Where did that idea come from?" he asked her flabbergasted.

"Seemed like a good idea at the time," she said somewhat worried that she had overstepped herself.

"Good idea?" Luke responded. "That was a great idea," he added excitedly. "You have missed your calling," he said to Addison. "You need to be in PR yourself. What a great idea," he repeated.

By nightfall, Addison's interview had been picked up by CNN, FOX, Entertainment Tonight, Access Hollywood and a host of other syndicated shows that promoted the entertainment industry. Late night TV hosts like Fallon, Colbert and Kimmel were all taking about it. Luke was being praised about taking a terrible situation and instead of making it "all about himself" turning it into something that could help thousands of people.

One of the talk show hosts suggested that food items be

dropped off with orange ribbons or stickers to promote anti-gun violence. Another issued a challenge that 220 tons of food be collected instead of the 220 pounds mentioned in the interview.

The challenge created so much media attention that the station erected a giant looking thermostat with 500-pound increments marking the way to the final 220-ton goal. They publicized a website e-mail and asked food banks around America to report how many pounds of food were donated daily.

Donations started pouring in. Other celebrities, trying to jump on the band wagon, used their Twitter, Instagram and Facebook accounts to promote the idea. The New York Times published updates on the progress made on the thermostat daily. Individuals posted hundreds of YouTube videos of themselves walking into food banks across America with bags of food. The whole idea became a media frenzy.

# CHAPTER TWENTY-THREE

"I need a nurse!" Henry barked into the phone.

He had called one of the numbers that had been programed into the cell phone that Miles had given him.

The person on the other end of the call was not sure how to respond, or with whom she was speaking with.

"If this is an emergency sir, you might want to hang up and call 911," was her reply.

"I don't need the police, and you're supposed to get me help if I need it." Henry responded.

"May I ask who I am speaking with?" A calm but confused Maggie Grace said to the caller.

"Henry Lukens," he replied. "I need some nurses right away."

Maggie had never spoken personally with Henry; she had only heard stories from former domestics she had placed with him about Henry's abusive behavior. She felt like she was getting a taste of that. After a few more carefully worded questions, Maggie was able to determine that Henry was looking for someone to come to the ranch to help take care of Luke when he was released from the hospital, and that he wanted private duty nurses for Miles while he was still in the hospital.

"I will be happy to help you with those requests," she told him knowing full well that she would be calling Addison the minute she hung up with Henry.

"Is there anything else that I can help you with?" she asked Henry.

After a few moments, Henry responded.

"Yes, I want a mature woman, like over fifty or a man nurse at the house. That Stephen would do fine," he said. "Needs to be someone that can lift a man easily," Henry added.

After some consideration, Maggie Grace thought that Henry was right, a male nurse would be the best choice. Addison didn't need any competition, she thought to herself.

Maggie Grace and Henry had determined that they only needed one nurse for the ranch. He felt that between him, Addison and the ranch hands they could fill in the rest of the time. He wanted someone to be there between noon and seven in the evening since those times most aligned with the hospital visiting hours and he wanted to be available to visit Miles. They had also determined that Miles should have three nurses, each with an eight-hour shift. Henry wanted to make sure that Miles had someone with him twenty-four hours a day.

"Do you have a preference for the nurses at the hospital?" Maggie grace asked.

"Yeah," Henry responded. "I want them young and pretty."

Henry felt at least that would brighten Miles' day a bit.

By the time the transport ambulance pulled into the

driveway, Glenn, the private duty nurse that Maggie Grace had sent over, was already in place. He helped the attendants from the transport company bring Luke into the house, got him settled into his bed, and changed and redressed Luke's leg wound. Luke slept a great deal of the afternoon.

Henry and Addison used that time to go back to the hospital to visit Miles. When they arrived, Beverly, one of the private duty nurses Henry had secured, was taking the blood pressure cuff off Miles' arm. They could tell that Miles was enjoying the singular attention that he was receiving. Henry asked Miles if he was satisfied with the other nurses and if there was one that he favored. Miles smiled and assured them that he was getting the best care possible from Beverly, Sue and Lisa.

Luke's first day at the ranch was rather hectic. A steady host of visitors came to see him. Raymond, Travis, and Dale started the procession of ranch employees who came up to the house to check on their boss. Luke's agent and some of the executives from the recording company came over bringing a satchel with hundreds of fan letters. His room was full of flowers and balloon bouquets sent from various CMA stars. His band members filed in and out for most of the day. By evening, both he and Henry's energy were spent. Thankfully, Glenn did a great job making the visitors somewhat limit their time.

The second day, things started to calm down and by the third, life was getting more normal. Addison thought that Glenn was a real-life saver, not only for Luke, but for her as well. She was beginning to feel the exhausting effect of caring for Luke, Miles and Henry. She loved all three of them, but countless nights of not sleeping, and the endless string of people coming into the house, left her drained.

Luke was still confined to his bedroom, but with Glenn's help he was starting to take short walks within his suite and with help was able to walk to the bathroom. Before Glenn left for the evening, he had returned Luke's dinner tray to the kitchen, helped him into his sleepwear and with his evening routine. Henry had brought in his favorite "Walker" DVDs for Luke to watch, and Glenn popped one into the player before he left.

After Henry went to bed, Addison looked in to check on Luke.

"Need anything?" she asked.

Luke smiled. "Have you seen these?" Luke didn't wait for an answer. "They're great," Luke said with an upbeat tone.

Addison rolled her eyes and smiled. A chip off the old block, she thought to herself.

"Any chance for some popcorn?" Luke asked Addison with a little boy smile.

Addison returned shortly with a hot bowl of buttered popcorn, lightly salted just the way Luke liked it.

"Would you put in the next DVD for me?" Luke asked, and then patted a space next to him on the bed.

"Hey, come here and watch this with me for a bit, I'll share my popcorn," Luke said to Addison.

She smiled. Addison climbed up onto Luke's large king size bed, the bowl of popcorn between them. At the start of each episode, Luke would join in singing the show's theme song that was sung by Chuck Norris.

*Cause the eyes of a ranger are upon you*
*Any wrong you do, he's gonna see*
*When you're in Texas, look behind you*

*Cause that's where the ranger's gonna be*

Just like his grandfather, Luke kept a running dialog of what was happening on the show.

"I don't get it," he said. "It is pretty obvious that Walker and Alex are crazy about each other, but neither one takes any action on it." Luke said. "Why doesn't he just admit it and marry her?" he added shaking his head as if he could not figure out what was holding the two characters back.

"I know exactly what you mean," Addison said with a sigh thinking to herself that she could totally relate to Alex Cahill.

By the third hour long segment, Addison's eyes were getting heavy. In the episode they were watching, Alex Cahill was on a raft with other victims that had been taken hostage with her. They had survived perilous white-water rapids and abuse from the criminal that had kidnapped them. Walker had made some kind of zipline and was hurling from the mountain side towards the raft to rescue Alex and the others. Addison never saw the ending as she drifted off to sleep.

When the show ended, Luke looked over at her and smiled. He was about to ask her if she wanted to watch the last episode on the DVD, but when he realized she was asleep, he did not want to disturb her slumber. He carefully pulled the bed comforter over her. He watched her for a few minutes and had a hard time resisting the urge to softly kiss her on the check. Instead, he used the remote to turn off the television and another to dim the lights.

In that sweet space of time between sleep and when alertness stirs the mind, Addison was dreaming about Ranger Walker's daring rescue. His strong arm was wrapped around

Alex who could feel his soft breath in her ear.

Slowly, Addison's eyes opened. She wasn't dreaming, but it was not Ranger Walker and Alex Cahill wrapped in a gentle embrace. Luke was sleeping next to her, and his strong arm was wrapped around her.

She didn't move. She didn't know what to do. She didn't want to move. She knew she should move. She took a deep breath and gently lifted Luke's arm. He stirred, and then drew her closer to him.

"Don't go," he softly whispered in Addison's ear. "Don't go," he repeated.

Addison did not want to go. The past week had been so painful. She was happy that Luke was safe, and she felt safe in his arms. She relaxed, her body melting into his.

"I just want to hold you close," he said. "Perfect gentleman, scout's honor," he whispered.

She knew in this quiet early morning hour, that he just needed to feel safe too. They drifted off again into a peaceful sleep.

Addison woke up when the aroma of hot coffee drifted through the hallway. She gently rolled over to see if Luke was awake. His eyes were opening.

"Pop's up," she quietly said.

He nodded his head.

You must know I love you, Luke thought to himself, but like the TV character he just could not get the words out.

"He'll be fine," Luke said.

Addison smiled softly as they gazed into each other's eyes. She wanted to kiss him, she wanted to be kissed by him, but all Luke did was return her smile.

"I better see if he needs anything," she told Luke as she slipped out from under the covers.

# CHAPTER TWENTY-FOUR

Henry did not like to fly, but he knew that it would have been too painful for Miles to manage the seven-hour drive between Nashville and Roanoke. Miles was still in a great deal of pain and his arm was in a sling. He probably should have stayed another week at the rehab center, but he thought a trip back to Botetourt would be better medicine, and he knew that staying with Henry on the family farm would give him time to rest and recuperate. Henry used the time on the plane to tell Addison stories about Roanoke. It was a good way for him to keep his mind off of flying.

"Do you know who Karen Carpenter was?" Henry asked Addison.

"Yeah," she replied. "My mom loved her music; she was an incredible singer. Died way too young." Addison added shaking her head slightly.

"Did you know she was on a TV show called the "Dating Game" once?" Henry asked her.

Addison shook her head no, she also had never heard of the Dating Game.

Miles interrupted saying, "It was an early attempt at Reality TV."

Addison acknowledged his comment with a nod, and Henry gave him an annoyed look.

"Don't mind him." Henry said to Addison as he continued, "Anyway, she had three fellows to pick from and the one she picked got to have a date with her, and the prize was a trip from LA to Roanoke."

Miles rolled his eyes and twirled his finger as if to say, "big deal," and then laughed to himself.

"Yes, you see, of all the places in the world, the big producers picked Roanoke." Henry said beaming. "They got to stay in the famous Hotel Roanoke. Maybe I will take you there for lunch while we are here." He told her.

"Luke smiled to himself as he continued to read the Golf Magazine he had picked up at the airport in Nashville.

"And Debbie Reynolds, you know who she was, right?" Henry continued.

Addison nodded and said, "Yes, and her daughter was Princess Leia."

Henry could not remember who Princess Leia was, but he knew that Debbie had been married a few times and assumed she had been a child that Debbie had when she was married to some prince. He remembered that Grace Kelly had married a prince, so why not Debbie he thought. Henry shrugged and then continued.

"Did you know that Debbie was married to a guy from Roanoke. She used to visit here a lot. It was a big deal when she came to town."

"I didn't know that." Addison said.

"And they got a great big star on the side of the mountain there. You won't believe how big it is. Bigger than some houses, over 100 feet tall, and they light it up every night. You can see the whole valley from there." Henry said enthusiastically. "Some people even go up there and get engaged," he said with a louder voice.

Miles leaned over and whispered to Luke, "Better be careful, Pop might be thinking about marrying Addison."

Luke looked at his friend and quietly replied, "I didn't realize you had a head injury too." He then returned to the article in the magazine that he had been reading.

Henry was still occupying Addison's attention with information about the Roanoke Valley. He told her that people liked to hike through there on the Appalachian Trail, and that the most beautiful views in the whole world were from the Blue Ridge Mountains.

"There is a lot of history there too," Henry continued. "In Botetourt, where we are going, well that's where Lewis and Clark started from. Back when the country was just wild and open, it stretched all the way to where Wisconsin is now." Henry told her.

Addison looked, surprised, and it was clear that she could not decide if this was fact or fiction.

Miles spoke up, "It's true, Fincastle was the start of the wild, wild west, and Pop would know, he worked twenty hours a day sweeping the general store and helping people change their wooden wheels on the wagon trains."

Henry was about to give Mile's a piece of his mind, when the captain of the small charter plane that was transporting Luke, Addison, Henry and Miles announced that they were approaching the Roanoke-Blacksburg Regional Airport and asked that they sit back and buckle their seatbelts.

When the plane landed and they entered the terminal, they traveled down the escalator to the main floor of the small airport. Normally, they would have rented a car, but with Luke's leg injury and Miles still in a sling they had decided to hire a driver, who was there waiting for them. He had a cart and went with them to the baggage claim area. Luke was doing his best not to use the cane that his doctor had insisted on. The driver loaded their luggage into the back of the luxury Chevrolet Suburban that Magnolia had arranged. Once settled in the vehicle, they headed towards the Lukens family farm in Fincastle, a small town in Botetourt County.

Since they had not flown commercial, the airport was fairly empty. Local reporters were not aware that they were arriving, which suited Luke just fine. The recent foodbank campaign had created a lot of attention and reporters had been clamoring for interviews. Over 400,000 tons of food had been collected nationwide and in Canada. More donations continued to come into the local agencies. A large number of fans had also sent in cash and check donations in get well cards addressed to Luke, hoping to score an autograph when he cashed the checks. He had turned all of that over to Pastor Rich and asked him to organize the best way to distribute those funds.

The farm had been in Henry's family for five generations. Pop had made Luke promise to never sell it, at least while he was living. Helen, and her granddaughter, Betty, lived at the farm now. Helen was nine years younger than her brother. Henry looked forward to seeing them, and to being closer to his beloved Alice. He liked seeing old friends and retracing some of the steps that he and Alice had shared. Betty had moved in with her grandmother last March after ending an abusive relationship that had brought her close to the brink of suicide. The farm had helped to heal her.

Henry's grandfather Henrich Lukens and his wife had left Germany in 1911. Like many Germans, they feared the growing power of Kaiser Wilhelm and his foreign policies. They had sailed to America in horrific conditions aboard a cargo ship. Huddled into filth and rat ridden cargo bays with other immigrants as they crossed the ocean, they dreamed of a better life in America.

With the onset of WWI, the American dream became a nightmare for German refugees. The US Government banned many aspects of the refugees' culture. They were not allowed to speak German, their children were ostracized and ridiculed in public schools and some families were separated or interned. Anti-German propaganda circulated in America and often resulted in fights and acts of violence against the poor immigrants.

Henrich and his wife worked hard and eventually, in 1918, were able to purchase a small track of land in Botetourt County located in Virginia. Henrich had been drafted by the US Government to serve in WWI against his native homeland. His wife, Hester, worked as a house servant with a family in Charlottesville until they were finally reunited.

There was a certain peacefulness about being at the Lukens' family farm. The people that lived in the small town had watched Luke grow up, and while they admired his success, they did not gawk or treat him any differently than they did when he was just plain old Jimmy, Henry and Alice's grandson.

Luke's great Aunt Helen and his cousin, Betty, were excited to see them. Luke could tell that Henry was glad to be home. It had been a long year. Betty's external scars she had endured from an abusive boyfriend had healed. With love and encouragement, the emotional scars were slowly dissipating, thanks in part to the counseling services her cousin Luke had arranged when he came to her aid last March.

It had been a challenge to persuade Henry to move to Nashville. He finally relented when Helen agreed to move back to the home where she and Henry had grown up. Helen and her husband, Roy, took care of the house and oversaw the running of the farm.

Luke had loved his Uncle Roy. He was a hard-working man with a jovial sense of humor. He was a great storyteller and usually had a wad of Kodiak in his mouth. Roy kept an old Campbell soup can in the cupholder of his truck to spit the tobacco in whenever they came over. Luke recalled that Gram would have a fit if she found him spitting in the grass or her garden.

Helen used to say that Uncle Roy was full of "tall tales," and Luke often thought that his ability to write the stories woven into some of his most popular ballads came from the inspiration he had gotten from Uncle Roy. His Uncle had passed away seven years earlier as a result of cancer in the esophagus.

Henry wanted the house to remain just as it had been when he shared it with Alice. He did not want anyone moving into their bedroom. He felt if he gave that up, he would never have a home to return to should he care to do that in the future. To appease him, Luke remodeled and added onto the part of the house that had been the original kitchen, so that Helen and Roy would have their own master bedroom on the lower floor. He added a large guest room above it for when their children came to visit.

Betty was the daughter of Helen and Roy's second child, Mark. She had moved in with her grandmother at a very low point in her life. Helen was sorry for the reasons, but happy to have the company. Betty was three years younger than Luke. Her father was employed by Advanced Auto and had moved to work at their headquarters in Raleigh, NC when Betty was only four.

Luke had not seen much of her growing up. He remembered her as always being a sweet child, but rather shy. She had grown into an attractive young woman, and Luke was happy that she was living with her grandmother. Betty busied herself with reading and cross stitch projects. She participated in the local bridge club that met at the town's recreation center. She loved to play the piano and she had a pleasant voice. Betty gave private piano lessons to area children and adults and had a part-time job at the small Methodist church in Buchanan playing on Sunday mornings. She was musical, like her cousin, but would not have ever dreamed of being a performer.

Betty and Addison became instant friends. Though quiet and reserved, Betty had a strength about her that grew from the abuse she had endured. She had come to terms with the evil that once controlled her and would never succumb to that fear again. Addison had not yet conquered her fears that something terrible could happen to those that she loved. She found comfort in Betty's peaceful nature.

Other than Maggie Grace, Addison had not really had a girlfriend to talk with and confide in over the past year. There were plenty of men around her at the ranch, but they did not have the same perspective on life that another woman would have.

Betty had graduated from Allegheny College in Meadville, Pennsylvania where she earned a Fine Arts degree in Music Education. The two women quickly learned that they shared a passion for the humanities and social sciences. Both loved the works of Austen and Bronte. They debated and discussed Austen's various protagonists and concluded, if someone had the whit and confidence of Elizabeth Bennet, the sensitivity of Elinor Dashwood, and the spiritual and moral instincts of Fanny Price, the world would know the perfect woman.

Betty shared some of her dreams about places she would like to visit, just to be able to walk where great composers and artists had once stepped. She talked about one day going to the Louvre in Paris or the British Museum in London and was in awe that Addison had been to both. They both admired Oscar-Claude Monet, the French Impressionist and it did not surprise Addison to learn that in addition to her musical talents, Betty was also an accomplished artist.

Holding an apple outstretched in his hand, Luke tried to coax Buster, the old mule that lives on the farm to come over to the fence. Buster had a mind of his own and age had not made the animal any less stubborn. Helen walked up to her great-nephew and smiled.

"Reminds me of when you were a little boy," Helen said. "He wouldn't come to you then, and he still won't come," Helen said with a laugh. "He's almost thirty years old. I don't think you are going to be teaching him any new tricks," Helen added sweetly as she rubbed her great-nephew's back.

Luke smiled at his aunt and tossed the apple as close to Buster as he could. The mule instantly snatched it up.

"Henry's mind is getting stronger. Looks better than he did last year too," Helen stated.

Luke thought for a minute. She was right. Pop was a lot sharper and stronger than he used to be. Maybe he didn't have dementia. Maybe he was just bored, Luke thought to himself.

"I think that Addie is good for him," Helen said. "I think she's good for both of you." She added as she turned away and headed back to the house.

# CHAPTER TWENTY-FIVE

Luke's band flew in a week later. To Henry's delight, Magnolia had booked the band members to stay at Hotel Roanoke, which was now part of the Hilton chain of hotels. Henry and Addison went with Miles and Luke to see them when they arrived, and to have lunch in the hotel's Pine Room. The beautiful Tudor-style hotel was built in 1882 and is on the National Register of Historic Places. Their Regency dining room specialized in French-inspired Southern cuisine.

Contestants for the Miss Virginia Pageant always stayed at the hotel. When Luke was younger, he and some of his buddies would hang out at the hotel on the day the young women arrived to get a glimpse of the beautiful girls. The arrival day was always spectacular. Many of the pageant girls planned grand arrivals with the hope that one of the local news photographers would feature them in the Roanoke Times. On Tuesday night, there would be a reception for the girls that was open to the public. His grandmother loved to go to that. The girls would be dressed in beautiful gowns and the city provided light refreshments. Although he pretended to protest, Luke never minded taking his grandmother for a close look at the contestants.

Right before he had enlisted in the army, one particular girl at the pageant had really caught his eye. Miss Roanoke Valley arrived at the hotel in a horse drawn carriage. He thought that Madison was one of the most beautiful girls he had ever seen. She was wearing an incredible, lightly tinted pink gown and looked like a princess. The entire crowd had been quite taken by her entrance, poise, and grace. Her brown hair was long and flowing, and she had the most gorgeous smile.

The newspapers loved the arrival and a photo of her waving from the carriage graced the front page of the local newspaper. At the reception, as the crowd shuffled through to shake hands with the girls, Alice told the young woman that her grandson was about to enlist in the Army. The girl was so kind and told him she would pray for his safety. She didn't win, although Luke thought she should have.

Luke never knew what had happened to her but she had been the inspiration of his first big hit, *Midnight with Madison* that he wrote while in the service. The words came to him on one of the lonely nights when the enemy was too close to allow for any sleep. It was Miles that encouraged him to put it to music. He wondered if Addison had ever been in a pageant. She certainly was pretty enough he thought.

Luke knew that the scholarships the girls receieved all came from donations, so he decided to ask Miles to find out how he could support the Miss Roanoke Valley Scholarship program. He wanted to establish a scholarship in memory of his grandmother. He knew she would like that. It was the least he could do he thought, since the song earned him the County

Music Association's award for New Artist. The first of many awards that he would earn through out his career. Years later he purchased the carriage that had brought her to the pageant and had it shipped to his ranch in Tennessee.

The band came to perform with him for Veteran's Day at the nearby Salem Veteran Affairs Hospital. This was the first performance they did together since the Nissan Center concert. The hospital's 206-acre campus was beautiful. President Franklin Roosevelt dedicated the facility in 1934. It serves Veterans that live in 26 counties in southwestern Virginia.

Usually from mid-November, after the CMA Awards, through Christmas, Luke gave the band a holiday hiatus to allow them to spend time with their families. They had all been off since September. Having to cancel so many concerts and refund the ticket costs was going to make a big dent in his revenue for the year. He knew it hurt the band members as well. He called his accountant and arranged for the band to all get their full salary and to still have the time with their families. That would mean starting up again right after New Year's and probably adding another month to their winter and spring tours.

He had been invited to be a guest on the CMA Country Christmas show, a guest host for the New Year's Eve celebration in Times Square and almost all the evening talk shows wanted him to make an appearance. A few asked him to bring his employee along that had first launched the successful food drive. He thought that might be fun if Addison would agree to it. He knew that Addison was supposed to have the month off and dreaded the thought of her going.

Things were so different now. Normally this would be the time they would be leaving the farm to head back to the ranch for a fun-filled holiday season. It would start off with the annual BBQ at his ranch and then he would be hosting and attending a lot of holiday parties. He really was at a loss for what to do. He could not expect Pop to go back to Nashville after only a two-week visit with his sister. He also knew that the trip here really took a toll on Miles, and he was not sure what Addison had planned. He knew he had to ask her.

The November weather was unusually mild. The afternoons had a warm breeze, and the evenings were just starting to get crisp. Betty suggested that they have a bonfire in the evening. They could grill hot dogs and hold the old metal popcorn popper over the wood. She could use the iron press to make fresh mountain apple pies over the hot coals. Everyone thought that was a great idea. Henry suggested to Luke that he take Addison on a hike around the farm while the weather was nice. He suggested they go down by the stream near the old shed where Henry's grandfather once had a still. Addison was intrigued by that and happy to go.

Sitting by the stream, Luke thought he would ask Addison what her plans were for the month.

"You know, you're officially off duty," he said tossing a small pebble into the stream.

"Are you trying to get rid of me?" Addison said with a slight smile.

"No, just curious if you had any plans," Luke replied.

She shrugged her shoulders.

"I haven't really thought about it," Addison said.

"Well," Luke said slowly, "if you could go anywhere, do anything, what would you like to do?"

Addison thought for a moment.

"Let's see," she said pensively. "Any place and anything," she repeated what Luke had asked, "well, after I got back from Alaska... and Hawaii...and the Serengeti... and, well a side trip to Sydney, Australia to see my parents, and of course eradicated every childhood disease and world hunger, I think I would spend my month at a beautiful ranch in Tennessee with the people I care about the most," Addison said, with her eyes lifting up toward Luke's face to see what his reaction would be.

Luke took a step closer to her and carefully brushed aside the strand of hair that the wind had blown over her eyes.

"What if some of the people that you care about didn't want to go to that ranch in Tennessee? What if some of them wanted to spend time at a farm in Virginia?" Luke said coming closer still.

"What if only one person wanted to go to Hawaii, or meet your parents, or be alone with you at that ranch in Tennessee," he said to her. "Would you still want to go?"

They were now only inches apart.

"I would," she answered softly, looking deeply into Luke's eyes.

"What if I was that one person," he said pressing his lips against hers in a kiss so deep, so passionate that it took her breath away.

"I would still want to go, I'd go anywhere," her words faded off as once again Luke pulled her body tight to his and kissed her again.

# CHAPTER TWENTY-SIX

Jake Harris was the star of the late-night television show, *Pillow Talk*. The show was extremely popular nationwide and was filmed in New York City. Jake was known for his great sense of humor, quick comebacks, and witty banter with his celebrity guests. He was thrilled that Luke Johnson had finally agreed to appear on his show.

"You know, Addison, we have been trying to get Luke Johnson on this show for a long time," Jake said addressing his comments to her.

The crowd applauds.

"But we didn't want just him, no, we wanted you, too," Jake added.

Addison blushes and looks very surprised.

"Well," he continues, addressing Addison. "Do you remember saying this when someone asked your name?"

A clip appears on the screen of Addison's interview at the hospital where she said,

"That's not really important, aren't we hear to talk about Luke?"

Jake Harris then said, "Well, we are here to talk about Luke, but your name is very important. You know, you are a very special young woman. You turned a terrible situation into a national movement."

The audience claps and cheers. Addison is not speaking, she just sits, feeling embarrassed and trying to smile.

"Because of your efforts, over 800,000 pounds, that's over 400 tons of food, was collected in less than a week to help our homeless and families in need."

The audience again claps. Then Jake looks at the audience, and says, "I'm just curious folks, how many of you donated to a foodbank because of this young woman, Miss Addison Albright, raise your hands up," he said, as the camera panned the audience. An overwhelming number of people had their hands up, for whom Harris, Addison and Luke clap.

"And do you remember when someone asked you this?"

The next clip was played.

"What is your relationship to Luke Johnson?"

Addison nodded her head, still looking a little embarrassed.

"I am just one of his employees," played on the tape.

"Well, I, for one, think you are much more than just one of his employees," said Harris.

The crowd cheers as Luke smiles and nods his head "yes."

"What do you say Luke, just one of your employees?" Harris asked Luke.

Luke clears his throat, and says, "Well, Jake you know she actually was hired by my grandfather, so officially, I think you could say she is his employee."

Listening back in Virginia to the show, Henry confirms

what Luke had just said to the family members gathered around the television with him.

"That's right boy, you tell them, Addison works for me. I hired her," Henry said beaming.

Miles looks at Betty and rolls his eyes, she in turn giggles.

"Well, I am glad we got that cleared up." Jake Harris says speaking into the camera making a "what the hell does that have to do with anything" kind of look.

"I just wanted to say that" Luke continues, "because it would not be ethical for someone to date an employee or fall in love with one."

He then reaches over and pulls Addison closer and gives her a kiss. The crowd goes wild, and Jake Harris is completely taken off guard.

"Holy Moly!" Harris shouted, "I never saw that one coming." He laughs, clapping his hands as the cameras zoom in closer on Luke and Addison.

"I guess that means you are no longer a free agent when it comes to the ladies, Luke," Harris says, and Luke nods affirmatively.

"Well, that explains a lot," as the camera does a close of Harris tapping one finger against the side of his forehead.

"Addison," Jake says reaching out and taking her hand in his. He then paused for a moment and looked over at Luke. "Is it okay if I hold," he stops talking but nods his head directing everyone's eyes to his hands holding Addison's.

Luke smiles and gives him the "ok" sign.

Turning his attention back to Addison, Harris continues, "Did you know that Luke Johnson only agreed to come on this show, if I could do something special for you?"

Addison looks at Luke and then at Jake, shaking her head to indicate that she had no idea what to expect next.

"Am I right that you love the New York Yankees?" David said.

"Yes." Addison replies enthusiastically.

"Am I right that you used to go to their games with your dad when you were younger? Am I right that you lived in New York for a while and went to as many games as you could? Am I right that you still watch, all the way out there in Nashville, as many Yankee games as you can on TV?"

Addison had been nodding yes to each of his questions.

"Well, before I tell you what your surprise is, I am curious," he said. "Do you have a favorite player?" he asked.

"Which season?" she replied.

"Which season!" he repeated loudly urging the audience to applaud.

"Well, let me ask you this," if you could meet any Yankee, from any year, living or dead, who would it be?

Addison smiled.

"Well, of course, all the greats, Gehrig, Mantle, Ruth, DiMaggio, Munson, Berra, Ford, Jackson, the Goose, Jeter, Rivera, and Torre," she said.

"Of course, of course," said Jake. "You weren't even born for most of those guys," he said with a laugh.

"True, but my dad loved all of them," she answered. "He even has a ball that Mickey signed," she added.

The host nods his head in approval and again the crowd cheers.

"I have to ask, are there any Mets that you like?

"Of course, Willie Mays he's their GOAT, and I guess Seaver,

Strawberry, Matlack and Reyes can't be overlooked," Addison said.

"No, they shouldn't be overlooked," the host replied making a wide eye expression into the camera.

"You know," he continued, "I'm really a Met's fan myself. I would have been really hurt if you didn't have at least one player that you thought was okay, you know?"

The crowd laughs and applauds.

"I heard you mention Joe Torre," he said, and Addison nodded.

"A lot of people think that Torre was a great manager, but he really was a great player too." Addison added.

"Well, funny you should mention him, because Luke here only agreed to come on my show if I talked a few Yankees into coming so you could meet them," Harris said to Addison.

Addison squealed, hugged Luke and clapped her hands.

"And it just so happens," Jake says to Addison and the audience, "one of the greatest New York Yankees managers ever, who lead the team to four World Series championships, had 2,342 hits as a player, was a catcher, first baseman, third baseman and former Major League Baseball's chief baseball officer from 2011 – 2020, Mr. Joe Torre is here with us tonight!"

The crowd is shouting, cheering, applauding, and standing as Joe comes out on stage. Addison is overwhelmed. He comes in, shakes Luke's hand and gives Addison a big hug. He then takes one of the five empty seats that stagehands had brought out.

"Well, we can't have a manager without a few players, can we?" Jake said as the audience clapped their hands.

"Let's welcome "Mr. October" Mr. Reggie Jackson!" The

crowd yells and cheers.

"Reggie hit 563 career home runs, including three consecutive ones at Yankee Stadium in game six of the 1977 World Series. He was an American League All-Star for 14 seasons, and the MVP in 1973, also receiving two World Series MVP awards and the Babe Ruth Award in 1977. The man who led his teams to first place ten times over his 21-year career."

While Jake shared the introduction, Reggie walked across the stage waiving at the audience. The crowd went wild when he stopped by Luke and pulled his cell phone out of his pocket to take a selfie with him and the music star. He then laughed and greeted Addison with a warm hug before shaking hands with Torre and taking the seat next to him.

"I think I also heard you mention this man's name," the host says. "Mr. Derek Jeter, 14 time All Star, five-time World Series Champion, World Series MVP, former NY Yankee team captain, all-time career leader in hits, ranked sixth in major League Baseball," his words are drowned out by the cheers of the crowd.

Addison is obviously overwhelmed. Derek kisses her on the cheek, shakes hands with the host and Luke and sits next to Jackson after giving him a hug and a pat on his back.

'I think we need to meet someone you really must have been cheering for this past season," Jake continues. "How about a warm welcome for Gleyber Torres, second basemen and shortstop for the New York Yankees, batting .275 with 62 home runs and 167 RBI's."

Again, the crowd is going wild! After he takes his seat with the other baseball giants. The camera man does a close up of Jake speaking to the audience.

"We have one seat left. Ohoooo," he smiles into the camera., "I wonder who it will be? We'll find out, right after this commercial break," he says with a smile.

Off camera, Addison is going back and forth between hugging Luke and Jake and walking over to shake hands again and talk with the players. They all return to their seats when the cameras come back on.

"Who do you think is next? Jake says to Addison.

"No idea," she answers back. "My heart is pounding," she adds trying to catch her breath.

"Well, yours is not the first woman to get their heart pounding, because next up is the New York Yankees most popular bad boy, Mr. Danny Perez. Playing left outfield, Batting a .260, with 11 home runs, 29 RBI's and 13 steels."

Danny comes out waving at the fans, ignores Luke and when he gets to Addison, picks her up and swings her in a circle, putting her down and giving her a kiss. He then shakes Jake's hand and slaps the hands of the other players as he passes them going to his seat.

"Hey Joe," Jake addresses his next comment to the former manager, "Do you think you could have whipped these fellows into shape, you know make them better ball players, maybe bring up their stats a little?"

Joe and the players all laugh, and Joe gives Jake a thumbs up.

"Well, what do you think? Are you surprised? Jake says to Addison while Luke and the crowd are still cheering and applauding. Addison nods an affirmation, but looks nervous and pale.

"Luke, did I get you what you wanted?" Jake asks his guest.

When things settle down, Jake says, "Well, the fellows here wanted to tell everyone about something special that has started up, and since Luke insisted on having some Yankees on the show, this seemed like a perfect time" he said.

"Joe, what can you tell us?" Jake said as the camera moved to take a closeup of Joe Torre.

"I just want to say I am happy to be here, happy that I can still walk across a stage at my age," said Joe, the crowd cheering again. "I just want to say that this young lady is a real inspiration."

"Thanks so much for being here and God Bless you, you look amazing," Jake replied.

"Derek? What have you guys got going on?" Jake asked.

"Well Jake, I am sure everyone here knows that all ball players want to make it home safely when they are running the bases."

Harris nods his head and a few members of the audience yell out, "Yes" and "We love you, Derek!" Derek smiles and waves, and then continues.

"Well, some of my major league brothers have formed a charity, called the "Make It Home Foundation." It is to help support our nation's heroes that put their lives on the line for us. Servicemen and women, members of police and fire departments and many others."

Reggie Jackson is nodding his head and then leans towards Jeter and adds,

"The money raised will help provide gear and equipment that will protect them and make their jobs easier so that they all can *make it home* to their families. In addition, there will be a major push to bring anti-violence, especially gun violence education to our schools,"

The audience stands up and gives a wild and supportive ovation.

"That's right," said Torres. "Did you know that 36,000 Americans are killed by guns each year? Over 100,000, just like our buddy Luke, are shot or injured."

Joe adds, "We'd like to see an all-star game this summer in Cooperstown to help fund the project."

After another round of questions, answers, and applauds, Jake turns to Danny and says, "Perez, your awful quiet tonight, you got anything to add?"

Danny Perez looked solemn. He stands for a moment and then walks over in front of Addison, who appears to be uncomfortable with the attention as she reaches out to hold Luke's hand.

"There are some things that I have done that I am not proud of," Danny says. "I have had wonderful opportunities, I am playing the game that I love, I should be the happiest man alive, but I am not. The one thing, the one thing that should have been the most important thing in my life I screwed up. I am truly sorry about that. I have really been working hard to change things, to get involved with worthwhile things like this charity, I want to prove that I am a new man," Danny states.

Everyone was silent. They did not know what to expect, or where he was going with this declaration. Suddenly, Danny pulled a small box out of his pocket and drops to one knee.

"I asked you once before and I blew it. I am asking you again, and I promise you I will be the man you want me to be, and I will dedicate my life to making you happy. Addison Albright, will you marry me? I am begging you," Danny pleaded.

The entire studio exploded with shouts, cheers, gasps and a wide range of emotions. Addison lost all color in her face and Luke jumped out of his seat. Jake Harris looked as shocked as Addison and the cameramen were all jockeying their equipment to get the best possible close ups of Danny, Addison and Luke.

At their homes, Maggie Grace choked on the white wine she had been sipping, Miles uttered an obscenity, and Henry jumped out of his seat.

"This is the guy?" Luke said looking at Addison.

She nodded her head yes. "Can we leave?" she said to Luke.

Luke looked at Danny. The conversation months ago he had had with Addison raced through his mind. This was the jerk that broke her heart. Danny Perez broke her heart, Luke thought to himself. And now he is proposing to her on national television! Luke was completely dumbfounded.

Luke's emotions went from shock to disbelief, to anger within seconds. Before anyone knew what was happening, Luke was out of his seat, throwing a punch at Danny, who returned it with a fist into Luke's right jaw. The two men ended up on the floor with all fists flying.

The TV host was trying to get the network to go to commercial, but the show's producers were insisting that the cameras stay on the two celebrities. Jeter and Torres were trying to separate the two, Addison was crying and shouting for them to stop. There had never been a more chaotic show on late night television.

Luke and Addison left the television studio as quickly as possible. They rode back to the hotel in silence. They did not want the driver to be privy to their private conversation.

"Why didn't you tell me Danny Perez was your former

fiancé?" Luke said to Addison while pacing the hotel room, holding an icepack against his face.

"I never thought the three of us would ever be in one place at the same time," Addison replied.

"And in New York City!" Luke added. "I got into a fistfight on national television in New York City with one of their golden boys," Luke exclaimed while pacing the floor.

"I think you won the fight," Addison said with a half-smile.

Luke stared at her for a moment. He then tried to smile, but the throbbing pain in his jaw prevented him from doing that.

Addison stood on her tip toes and carefully kissed his cheek and then softly kissed his lips.

"I don't know if I won the fight," Luke said, "but I do hope I won the girl."

"No contest," Addison replied and kissed his swollen cheek again.

After a long conversation on the phone with Addison and Luke, both Henry and Miles calmed down.

The event made top headlines across the nation in every newspaper, newscast, magazine and social media.

Rival late-night shows talked for days about the new "anti-violence' program announced by the MLB players, and then showed slow motion footage of Danny hitting Luke. Another one of the shows had footage of baseball games clearing the benches when teams started fighting with each other, and then showed shots of Torres and Jeter leaping out of their seats to break up the brawl.

A *Top Ten Ways Not to Propose to Someone* list went viral on the internet. Radio stations repeatedly played songs that featured rednecks fighting over women and broken hearts. On the plus side, Luke's agent was ecstatic because his music sales had reached an all-time high.

Before leaving New York, Luke asked if he could come back on the evening show. The producers agreed. When he came out, the crowd was not sure how to react. Jake was wearing blue colored protection headgear and on his table were three plates. The first one had a large raw steak, the second a bag of frozen peas and the third a large ice pack.

"I just wanted to be prepared," he said as he shook Luke's hand. The two men laughed and sat down.

"And later in the show, the Palisades Junior High Badminton Team will be here," Harris said jokingly.

"That's okay, right?" he asked Luke looking at the camera with a fake look of concern on his face. "No grudges with any twelve-year-old badminton players?" Jake asked his guest.

The crowd exploded with laughter.

The two men tried to keep it lighthearted as much as possible, but Luke spent most of his time apologizing for his actions. He said he felt badly that a wonderful program like "Make It Home" was launched under these circumstances and he pledged a sizable donation to the Foundation. Luke was asked a number of questions about Addison, all of which he evaded. When asked about Danny Perez the only comment that Luke made was,

"All I can say, if he ever wants to give up baseball, I could use him on my security staff."

The crowd roared with laughter.

Harris produced an envelope and handed it to Luke. A closeup from one of the cameras showed two season tickets for the Mets. Jake then told Luke that they were a gift from Steinbrenner.

The audience again went wild with laughter.

The next morning, Luke surprised Addison with tickets to Sydney and made a joke about the two of them needing to get out of town. He had purchased the tickets, long before the television debacle, to surprise her with a trip to visit her parents in Australia. He was anxious to meet them, and he planned to propose to her as soon as he asked her father's permission. The return flight had a stopover in Hawaii where he planned to pop the question.

# CHAPTER TWENTY-SEVEN

Henry was enjoying the late fall weather on the farm. He and Helen shared stories and memories from their childhood and Helen cooked a number of dishes that their mother used to make. That pleased Henry a great deal. Some old neighbors came to visit, and Henry busied himself with a few projects in the barn. Sometimes he would go on short walks around the property and relive memories that he and Alice shared together. Almost daily he had Helen drive him over to the cemetery where Alice, John and Roy rested.

The farmhouse where Henry and Helen grew up, and he later shared with his wife, Alice, had been built in the mid 1800's and improved by each generation that lived in it. The original farmhouse had two small stories. To the left of the entry was a bedroom with a small closet and a fireplace. The stairs to the second story separated the bedroom from the parlor. Through a covered breezeway from the living room was the kitchen where, at the far end, there had been a hand pump for well water. A large wood burning cook stove had been used to prepare meals and heat the bath water.

Henry's grandparents used the downstairs bedroom, and their seven children shared the other two. The four boys slept in one of the rooms and their three sisters shared the other. On cold winter nights they shivered under layers of handsewn quilted blankets. In the summer, the children would sometimes sleep out on the upper porch they accessed through a window at the end of the hallway.

In the 1940's Henry's father had a coal furnace installed. The tiny iron door where deliverymen would shovel the coal into a chute that led to the basement could still be seen on the outside. Henry had converted that to an oil furnace in the 1960's. Luke converted that to an energy efficient heat pump and central air conditioning.

One part of the basement still had an old single toilet and a crude shower where young John and his father would clean up after doing chores around the farm, before coming up to the main part of the house. Neither had been used for years, but Henry had insisted that they not be disconnected in case there was an emergency and he needed them.

The main house now was a large white, 3,558 square foot two story building with a full walk-up attic and semi-finished basement. On the front of the house, was a large wrap around porch with four rocking chairs and a glider that two people could share. The back porch was enclosed with windows that allowed for natural sunlight to illuminate the room. Helen used that space to fill card tables with African violets and other plants she had moved inside to shelter them from the coming winter.

The main floor of the home had a remodeled kitchen with custom cabinets, stainless steel appliances, and a large island that six people could easily sit around. There was a family size dining room, a living room and a front parlor. Luke had converted the original kitchen area into the suite for Helen. Her suite included a master bedroom with a full bath and a large walk-in closet.

Luke had insisted that Miles use the bedroom above Helen's so that he would be as comfortable as possible during his recovery.

Henry had taken the bedroom furniture that he and Alice shared with him to Nashville. Per Henry's request, the single bed and dresser his son John had used, which had been stored in the attic, was moved into Henry's bedroom for his use when he came back to the farm for visits.

The 150-acre farm included a six-stall barn with ten acres fenced in for horses with three paddocks. There was also a large pond that watered the farm's livestock as well as the deer, birds and other wildlife found in the area. Luke's ancestors had grown tobacco on the farm. Most of the fields now produced corn and hay. A neighboring farmer, who had been a longtime family friend, rented the land for $1.00 a year plus the responsibility of checking in on Helen and helping her with anything that she needed. Luke had installed a swimming pool behind the house.

Miles still needed some help with his recuperation. Helen encouraged Betty to assist him. Miles' doctor wanted him to do some exercises to help bring strength and mobility back to his shoulder. It was still difficult for him to drive. He was right-handed, and the injury had been to his right shoulder which made simple tasks using his left hand more difficult.

To pass long afternoons, Miles would listen to Betty practice on the piano. She played a wide variety of music which he enjoyed. They would sit together and read books, play some board games or cards and talk about current events. As time passed, the two of them began to have long and personal conversations.

One afternoon, Betty shared with him information about the abusive relationship she had been in. Her former boyfriend had been very controlling, isolating her from family and friends. He would be verbally cruel towards her with insults and put-downs about her appearance and call her stupid.

"He made me feel like I was worthless," she confided to Miles. "He always wanted to pick a fight with me. First, he started accusing me of having affairs with other men. When that started, he began punching holes in our walls or breaking things. After that, he would hit me. He told me he would kill my family if I said anything. He said he didn't want to hurt me, but it was my fault, and it was his job to teach me a lesson. I guess I was stupid," Betty said. "I believed him, and I stayed with him."

As the days went on, Miles and Betty seemed to grow even closer. He complimented her on her piano playing. He thanked her repeatedly when she offered to help him button his shirts or pull on his boots. She even helped him wash his hair one morning in the kitchen sink. What started out as helpful tasks of assistance began to turn into sincere and genuine acts of kindness.

During one of their quiet conversations, Miles confided to Betty stories from his past, and some of the pain his early life bestowed.

"My folks were junkies. Half the time they were too stoned to even know I was there. We never had food in the house. Sometimes I wouldn't have anything to eat for days."

"That's terrible," Betty said softly. "How old were you?"

"I don't know," Miles replied, "Maybe four, maybe five," he answered.

"When I got a little older, maybe seven or eight, I used to wish they were dead," Miles said seriously. "Then when they died, I thought it was my fault."

"How did it happen?" Betty asked.

"Car wreck. At least they didn't take anyone else out with them," Miles said shortly.

"You can't blame yourself for that. You're lucky you didn't get killed, too," Betty told him.

"I wasn't with them. I was home watching something on TV, and they forgot I was there. They just left, and never came back," Miles said solemnly.

"What happened then?" Betty asked.

"Foster homes, one after another until I was old enough to join the Army, and then I got out of there," Miles told her.

"Were they bad?" Betty inquired with sympathy in her voice.

"Some were better than others," he told her. "But you know, for the most part, they all tried. I did everything possible to make them hate me. I broke every rule they had until they finally sent me off to another home. I just was not an easy kid to love, I guess I just didn't feel like I was worth loving."

"You are, don't say that" Betty said reaching out and touching his arm.

"Sometimes I feel like I should send them all something, kinda like an apology. I don't think they would believe that I turned out okay," said Miles.

"You're better than okay," Betty said with a smile. "How did you cope?" she asked.

Miles laughed. “Believe it or not, for a long time I wrote poetry.”

“Really?” Betty said somewhat surprised. “I wish I could read some of it. When was the last time you wrote anything?”

“Right after Gram died. I wrote a bunch of stuff then,” he said meekly.

“Where is it?” she asked him.

“I don’t know,” he replied.

Miles was feeling a little uncomfortable. It had always been hard for him to share his feelings. He had some regrets about opening up. It made him feel vulnerable.

With Thanksgiving a couple of days away, Helen had Miles and Betty busy working in the kitchen. They peeled apples for pies, pureed pumpkin, baked bread and helped with other dinner preparations. Miles’ arm was starting to get stronger, and he demonstrated his skills by lifting a five-pound bag of sugar over his head. Henry was a little sad that Luke and Addison would not be with them for the holiday, but they were still with her parents in Australia.

After dinner, Miles and Henry settled into comfortable chairs to watch football. Helen and Betty finished the dishes, and with no interest in the game, they sat and talked together in the kitchen. Helen had noticed a difference in her granddaughter. Her mood was lighter, and she seemed happier than she had been since her arrival last winter.

Later that week, Helen asked Betty to go up to the attic to retrieve some boxes of items that once belonged to Helen’s mother. She thought it would be a good time for her and her brother to sort through them while he was visiting. Betty spent a good part of the afternoon trying to find the items that her grandmother requested.

In one corner of the large, open room were stacks of boxes. Most were labeled "Jimmy." There was one labeled "Miles," that caught her eye. She was curious about what had been stored in his box and gently removed the lid to peer inside. She felt some guilt going through the mementos that had been saved for Miles. Army medals, a few photographs, a couple of non-noteworthy report cards from high school, some old medical papers. Really nothing that illustrated a life of happiness or accomplishments. At the bottom of the box was a worn spiral notebook. She started to flip through it and realized it was some of the poems that Miles had mentioned.

The next few days, Betty seemed distracted when she played the piano. Instead of a familiar song, she practiced different keys and melodies. Her hands danced across the keyboard alternating between forte and pianissimo strokes until a melody was created that pleased her.

"What are you working on?" Miles finally asked her.

"I read something that I really liked, and I wanted to put some music with it," she replied.

"Care to share?" he asked her.

Hesitantly, she started to play, softly singing some of the words she had read in the notebook she had found in the attic.

*"With the courage of Eagles*
*The heart of the Dove*
*The Wisdom of Owls*
*She soars high above*
*The great river she crosses,*
*And on the banks far beyond*

*Her new home awaits her,*
*Old friends she has found.*
*I often hear whispers*
*Her voice in the air*
*When the sun warms my shoulders*
*I know she is near."*

Her voice faded off as her gentle touch of the keyboard created a decrescendo at the end. She was afraid to look at Miles. Would he remember those words? Would he be angry that she had read them? Would he be angry that she blended his beautiful gift with hers?

There was silence for a few moments. Finally, Miles came over and sat next to her on the piano bench.

"Where did you find that?" he asked her.

She told him about the boxes in the attic.

"I didn't know they were up there," he replied.

"Are you mad?" she asked, afraid of what the answer might be.

Miles looked at her for a few moments. Shaking his head, he then leaned closer to her, and kissed her. He had kissed plenty of other women, but this was different. With other women, his only thoughts had been about his pleasure. With Betty, he wanted desperately to make her happy, to make her feel loved and needed. He had never felt this way about anyone before.

Over the next few weeks, they worked together, putting the rest of the poem to music. Betty convinced Miles that they should share it with Luke when he and Addison returned from their trip.

# CHAPTER TWENTY-EIGHT

Addison and Luke returned to Botetourt the week before Christmas. No one was really surprised when she showed them the beautiful diamond engagement ring that Luke had given her after he had asked her father's permission for them to marry. Everyone, especially Henry, was thrilled with the news. Lively conversations carried through the entire holiday about dress styles, bridesmaids, bridal showers, reception halls and guest lists until Henry expressed that he had heard enough of the plans.

Pop had enjoyed his time with his sister and grandniece but even he was ready to return home to Tennessee. He missed seeing Raymond and the other guys. He missed his daily routine and, as much as he loved his sister, he was ready for life to be back to normal.

They all planned to head back to Brentwood at the end of December. To everyone's surprise, Miles announced that he planned to stay a little longer. In his weeks of recuperation, he had grown exceptionally close to Betty. What had started as a casual friendship had blossomed into deep feelings for each other. Helen marveled to herself how one terrible injury could heal two lost souls.

The newspapers, tabloids and talk show hosts were consumed with the upcoming nuptials. Photographers stalked the ranch and every movement that Addison made beyond the security of the driveway gate. Dale was assigned to be with Addison every second when she left the ranch and Travis was her full-time driver. Photographers and hordes of fans tried to get her attention. Hundreds of congratulatory letters were sent to her, along with some harassing ones that did not like the idea of Luke getting married.

The guest list was enormous and read like a "who's who" list of top country entertainers. Of course, Maggie Grace would be her matron of honor, Betty would be a bridesmaid, and Maggie's little daughters were going to be flower girls. Miles naturally would be Luke's best man and Pastor Rich was asked to perform the wedding ceremony. Addison's parents would arrive about a week before the wedding and her father would walk her down the aisle.

Luke and Addison had decided to hold the wedding at the ranch. They picked the first Saturday in April, a little over a year from when Addison had first arrived and helped to transform Henry back into the strong, confident man he used to be, and helped to mellow out the arrogant, condescending man that Miles had become.

Maggie Grace's company had taken care of all the details. Her staff arranged for the caterers, the valets to park the cars, the security to protect the assembled stars and to ward off invasive paparazzi. As hard as Addison tried to keep the event low key and simple, she soon learned that marrying a star opened every decision to public commentary and scrutiny.

A large white tent had been erected in the field across from the pond. Hundreds of white carnations and flickering candles floated across the water behind the platform erected to hold the bridal party. As Luke, Miles and Travis stood waiting, Raymond navigated the horse drawn carriage that Addison had first noticed by the barn when she came to live at the ranch. The carriage was encased with beautiful flowers as it carried her and her father to the long white runner waiting for her to walk on towards her groom.

Betty led the procession followed by Maggie Grace. The darling little girls followed their mother, tossing white rose petals down the aisle. Addison looked beautiful. Her dress was designed by Carolina Herrera. It had a strapless bodice with intricately embroidered overlays. Gentle rouching around the waist accentuated Addison's slender features. She carried a bouquet of beautiful white lilies and little white flowers had been intricately woven into the band on her wedding veil. Luke looked exceptionally handsome in his black tuxedo.

The ceremony and the celebration that went with it lasted the entire day. A full course luncheon was served with a large buffet in the evening. In addition to the contracted musicians, many of the guests took turns playing guitar or singing. Luke and Addison changed into comfortable clothes mid-afternoon. Their guests had been encouraged to bring a change of clothes as well.

Luke looked much more relaxed in his blue jeans and cowboy hat. Addison wore a white jumpsuit. Guests enjoyed trail or wagon rides, four wheeling in jeeps, swimming in the pool, boating in the lake and of course they all danced. About nine in the evening, guests were invited to send Wish Lanterns into the sky. Fireworks were shot off over the pond about ten that evening after which, Luke and Addison climbed into a large limousine as they passed through a long line of sparklers as handfuls of bird seed was gently tossed at them by the well-wishers that had stayed for the entire day.

The happy couple rode around Nashville for about an hour. Miles and Betty met up with them and they climbed into his CJ7 and drove back to the ranch. By the time they got back, the guests had cleared out and Mr. & Mrs. James Lukens spent their wedding night at the place they both loved the best, in their own bedroom. They planned to fly to a private island in the Caribbean the next day to enjoy two full weeks of rest and relaxation before Luke headed out for his spring concert season.

In early July, Luke, Henry and Addison all returned to the farm in Virginia. This time, they would celebrate a second wedding. Miles and Betty were to be married in the same little church where Henry and Alice had exchanged vows many years before.

On the day they arrived at the farm, Henry asked Luke if he would drive him over to the cemetery. Luke was happy to do so. A small memorial bench had been erected at the foot of Alice's grave. Henry would often sit there and have private conversations with his late wife and son. Today, he sat with Luke.

"I don't guess you ever will move back to the farm," Henry said to his grandson.

"I love it here," Luke said, "but no, I don't ever see myself moving back."

Henry nodded.

"I always wanted this farm to stay in the family, you know," Henry said to Luke.

"What would you think," Henry said pausing, "If we signed the deed over to Miles and Betty as a wedding present?"

Luke's grin answered his grandfather's question.

"I think that would be perfect!" Luke said sincerely. "It will stay in the Lukens line through Betty, and you know, Pop, I think this honestly was the first real home Miles ever had."

Henry nodded in agreement.

"I think it would make your grandmother happy, too," Henry said, tearing up a bit. "Miles will watch over her when I am not here, and maybe me, too, someday," Henry said reflectively.

Henry, Addison and Luke all stayed with Helen while Miles and Betty enjoyed a trip to London and Paris. Betty was finally able to visit the museums she had dreamed about seeing. When they returned, Addison helped Henry pack his things for their trip back to Tennessee. She helped him empty his drawers, folded his shirts and when she went to the bedroom closet he had shared with Alice for their long and loving marriage, she could not help but notice a faded blue apron with little white flowers hanging on a small hook.

END

# ACKNOWLEDGEMENT

Kathryn would like to acknowledge her sister, Betty Youmans who she credits as being her "best editor, proof reader and supporter" and her daughter Madison VanDuyne who she credits as being her best "idea bouncer" and "cheerleader"

# ABOUT THE AUTHOR

## Kathryn Hartz Beard

Kathryn Beard earned her Doctorate from the University of Virginia and completed her undergraduate work at Syracuse University. She was raised in upstate New York and currently lives in Botetourt County in Virginia Her husband Dale grew up on a farm in Southwest Virginia. Dr. Beard enjoys listening to country music, traveling, MLB and spending time with her children and grandchildren.